RENEE

Book Seven in the Apron Strings Series

OTHER BOOKS IN THE SERIES

Polly (1920s) by Naomi Musch

Nellie (1930s) by Amy Walsh

Priscilla (1940s) by Jenny Knipfer

Beatrice (1950s) by Patti Wolf

Joann (1960s) by Donna Jo Stone

Cynthia (1970s) by Jessica Marie Holt

Cassie (1990s) by Lisa Howeler

Kristen (2000s) by Dawn Klinge

Paige (2010s) by Regina Walker

Maddie (2020s) by Dawn Kinzer

Corner Room Books, Salisbury, North Carolina, USA

For more information on this book and the author visit: www.sandraardoin.com.

Print ISBN: 979-8-9905848-0-8
Cover design and formatting by Samantha Fury
Editing by Lynne Tagawa

Other Books by Sandra Ardoin

Contemporary Romance

Hidden Veil Hometown Series
A Musician's Heart
A Horseman's Mission

Love at Christmas Inn Series
Love in Second Bloom
Leaving the Past Behind
Lost in Winter's Wonderland
Box Set: *Longing for Second Chances: Three Second Chance Romance Novellas*

Historical Romance

Widow's Might Series
Unwrapping Hope
Enduring Dreams
Rekindling Trust

Barnes Brothers
The Yuletide Angel
A Reluctant Melody

A Love Most Worthy
Daphne's Day Out

Renee

Apron Strings Series

Book Seven

Sandra Ardoin

Corner Room Books

Two are better than one, because they have a good return for their labor: If either of them falls down, one can help the other up. But pity anyone who fallsand has no one to help them up.

Ecclesiastes 4:9-10

A word from *Mrs. Canfield's Cookery Book*:

Dear Friends,

How glad I am that this cookery book has made its way into your hands. I hope it will become more than a collection of recipes, and that in your home it will help foster an environment filled with love, family, friends, and of course, good food. Cooking and baking are more than necessary skills for a homemaker. They can be an art form. They can be a ministry. Most of all they can be a way to show love.

Food is an essential and everyday part of our lives, but it can be so much more. I hope through the pages of this book you will find not only instruction but also inspiration for your body and your soul.

Happy cooking and baking! May you give and receive many blessings through your efforts.

Warmly,

Mrs. Clara Canfield

CHAPTER ONE

North Carolina, July 1986

"One day . . ." Renee Burnette shoved the permed curls away from her face. "One day we'll be out of this cramped cracker box."

One day couldn't come soon enough to provide her son with what she never had growing up.

"What'd you say, Momma?" Her six-year-old gawked at her from the sofa a few feet away, the locks of his brown hair hanging over his forehead.

Each day he looked more like his father with those bright brown eyes and rosy cheeks. Joy and sorrow mingled inside her at seeing the way her husband lived on in his son. "It was nothing, Travis."

She searched for an open spot on the counter for her skillet. Sink. Stove. Refrigerator. In-between appliances, the apartment's architect had tossed in a couple of small counter spaces—yellow islands, each only large enough to hold a toaster or coffee maker.

With a half-twist right then another one left, she almost laughed, imagining Julia Child trying to film a television show in this tight galley kitchen.

Her gaze latched on to the clock sitting on the TV cabinet. She gasped and dropped the pan with a clatter onto the stovetop.

How had time slipped away so quickly? Washing dishes would need to wait until tonight.

"Come on, honey bear. We're late."

"But I can't find my shoes."

"Look under your bed."

Travis eyed her as if she'd lost her mind. She cringed. Maybe she had lost it, since her baby had no bed of his own, not a normal one. Not since they moved into this one-bedroom apartment. Every night, he slept on the pull-out sofa.

She whipped off the white bib apron with its navy and red vertical pinstripes and hung it in the tiny closet near the front door. Grabbing the purse hanging off one of the two chairs at the small kitchen table, she hurried to her son, frowning at his shoeless feet. "Did you look for your shoes in the bedroom? Did you put them under my bed?"

"There's no room under there."

She couldn't argue with that. The boxes stashed under the double bed occupied just about every inch of floor space. No room for dust bunnies, at least.

"Well, they must be somewhere around here. This apartment isn't big enough to hide a gnat."

Though she generally kept it neat, she also had a talent for giving others the impression she'd found a place for everything and that everything resided in its place. Ha!

The only other apartment complex in the town of Glenboro offered two-bedroom units at no more rent than she paid now, but it wasn't kept up well, and she'd read too many newspaper articles involving visits by the police. She wouldn't sacrifice her son's safety for a few more square feet. Here, Renee had less room but nice neighbors, including the elderly woman across the covered walkway and her boss, who lived two buildings over.

A two-bedroom apartment in this complex was out of the

question, though. The less money she spent plus the more she saved equaled a house of their own, a firm and stable foundation for Travis. No more moving from place to place like she had done growing up and after her marriage. As an Army brat, she knew marrying one of her father's soldiers would require her to continue the nomadic lifestyle she hated. But she couldn't ignore love.

Renee slipped into her blue and yellow plaid blazer. "If we don't hurry, I'll be late to work. Grab your Sunday shoes and your coat, and let's go." Renee looked forward to August when Travis would begin school. It would cut down on the daily childcare expense.

"But, Mama, I want to wear my KangaROOs."

"I know, honey, but we don't have time to look for them right now."

"Grandma will be mad if I lost them."

The shoes with the jumping kangaroo on the side had been a birthday gift three months ago from her in-laws, and yes, her mother-in-law wouldn't be happy to discover he'd lost them. "They're here somewhere. We'll look again tonight."

Though the valley town near the southernmost edge of the Blue Ridge Mountains was growing, Glenboro remained small enough that she faced little traffic to slow her down. Five minutes after pulling out of the apartment complex, Renee parked at the curb in front of the daycare center. No other cars nearby, just her Oldsmobile Omega. No other children in sight.

She ran around the front of the car to the back door on the passenger side. Travis had already released his seat belt, something he'd begun doing since turning what he called "The Big Six."

"What have I told you about waiting until I get to you?"

"But I'm gonna be in first grade pretty soon. I don't want

all the kids thinking I'm a baby."

Well, you are. You're my baby.

With no time to argue, Renee exhaled a sigh, opened the door, and helped him onto the sidewalk. She handed him the E. T. lunch box she'd bought secondhand at a yard sale.

Her baby might consider himself grown up already, but there was one thing she wasn't about to give in on yet. "Kiss, please." After receiving a quick and warm peck on the right cheek, she looked up to find the director, a fellow member of her Culinary Capers group, watching from the doorway. "You'd better go inside."

While Travis entered the church building, Renee controlled an impulse to snap her fingers. She'd forgotten it was her turn to supply the dessert recipe and ingredients for the upcoming Capers meeting. Part culinary, part Bible study, and part therapy session, half a dozen women from her church made up the cooking club. She never missed a meeting if she could help it.

What would she plan for them to make? Well, she had two days and would decide later, when she wasn't running late to work.

Renee trotted to the driver's side of the sedan, climbed in, and pressed the gas pedal a little harder than she would normally. It wasn't as though she made a habit of getting her son to daycare late. Still, the guilt rose and she chastised herself for being irresponsible this morning.

A few minutes later, she pulled into the parking lot behind the one-story real estate office downtown. As she rushed toward the building, her focus on slipping the car keys into her purse, she bounced off a wall—a warm masculine wall. Drakkar Noir cologne—herbs, spices and a woodsy scent announced her boss's presence. He always wore just enough to notice, but not so much it overwhelmed.

Strong hands clasped her arms to keep her upright. "Good morning, Renee."

Her gaze found its way upward. Gregory Marcus Holmes. A man with a smiling face and a sunny disposition. And those eyes! Sparkling blue-gray, paired with a head full of thick, nearly black hair. She knew better than to sigh, but sometimes she couldn't help herself. Fortunately, she controlled her wayward expression this morning. Barely.

He released his hold but didn't walk away.

"I'm sorry, Mr. Holmes. We got a late start, then Travis couldn't find his shoes, and I had nowhere to put the dirty skillet." She inhaled a deep breath. "You didn't need to know all that."

Renee felt like a fool, first for running into him, then running on about nothing and taking up his time. What must he think of her?

His wide smile showed off a row of glorious straight white teeth. "It's more believable than 'The dog ate my homework.'"

"I don't have a dog." Mainly, because she had no yard for one to run around in. "But when I get one, I'll remember that excuse."

As Renee backed away, he lost that sunshine smile. Great. Somehow, she'd offended him. Because she didn't seem to appreciate his joke? She had. But she couldn't be too informal with him. She needed this job.

Now all business—all boss—he opened the door at the rear of the building for her. "After you."

"Yes, sir. Thank you."

Manners, kindness, good looks. More than once, Renee had wondered why he hadn't married. Of course, he could be divorced. She'd never really inquired, but something like that would have been whispered about.

"You're not late, you know."

No, but she was later than usual, and she tried hard to prove herself a dependable and capable employee. Greg Holmes, the owner of a growing and successful company, could afford to be a little late. He didn't have a child whose future depended on his ability to remain employed.

Soon.

She had scraped and scrounged for over two years, paying off debts like her car with the small amount of life insurance she'd received after her husband's death. The balance in her savings account proved she'd made progress. If all went well—*Please, God*—she would reach her goal within the next twelve months.

Travis deserved a house in which to grow up, a yard to play in, maybe even that dog to eat his homework—the type of permanent place *she* never had growing up.

* * *

Renee raised the lid of the photocopier, pulled out the eleven-by-fourteen sheet of paper, and carried the original and the copy to her desk. She smiled at the builder standing there, the potential purchaser of a lot in the Mountain Hollow development. She outlined the remaining available lots with a red marker, stapled it to the latest price list, and handed it to him. "There you are, sir. I hope you find the perfect lot for the next house you'd like to build. I understand your last one sold quickly."

"Yes, it did. Greg has a hot development on his hands. When will he begin the next one?"

"I can't say for sure, but I know we'll contact you."

"Good." As he walked toward the reception area, he folded the paper. "Thanks, Renee. As always, you're a gem."

A lightness filled Renee's chest, and she glanced down the hall in the direction of her boss's office. He probably sat at his desk with his head bent over a pile of paperwork. Renee truly enjoyed helping the builders, but she couldn't deny a desire for Mr. Holmes to have heard the compliment she'd received. But he was too far away.

A throat cleared. "If I were single, I'd look, too."

Valerie Sargeant's quiet voice drew Renee's gaze to the doorway leading into the reception area. Her friend had arrived already?

Renee glanced at the clock—yes, it was lunchtime. She grabbed her purse. "How long have you stood there?"

Val leaned closer and whispered, "Long enough to see you mooning over your boss—your single, handsome boss."

Renee's face heated knowing Val wasn't completely wrong. With her desk sitting in the open at the bend of an L-shaped hallway, anyone could overhear, especially the receptionist. Renee glanced around, then responded with her own whisper. "Don't be silly. I was not thinking about him, not in the way you're making out."

"I'm not the one looking as though I want to make out." Val's eyebrows bounced and she laughed. "Oh, please. Every time he enters the bank, we have to resuscitate at least two tellers."

Despite herself, Renee grinned. "Valerie Sargeant, shame on you. I was only . . ." She didn't want to discuss her hope of impressing Greg Holmes with her work ethic. Not here. "Are you ready for lunch?"

Normally, Renee brought her lunch and ate in the small break room near the building's rear door. That morning, Val had called and suggested they go to Gully's Restaurant down the street for the soup and sandwich special. Renee had almost declined, but something in Val's voice had stopped her. She'd heard the distinct ring of desperation.

Sometimes, her friend needed time away from her job at the bank and the kids and the responsibilities of home. Renee's sandwich, made from last night's leftover meatloaf, would still be good tomorrow. "Let's go."

With a wave to the receptionist, she and Val walked out the front door and into an already hot July day. Since meeting at church when she first moved to Glenboro—almost six months before her husband Steve passed—Renee and Val had become more than fellow members of the same congregation. Renee considered Val her best friend—a friend who had assisted her, consoled her, and cried with her throughout her adjustment to widowhood. It was Val who talked Renee into joining the Culinary Capers Club and Val who first heard of the job opening at Holmes Real Estate Developers. Renee hadn't had such a good friend since elementary school.

"I hope autumn comes early this year. I'm already dying to see the leaves turn on the mountains." Val fanned her face with her hand. "It's supposed to reach the low nineties today."

"Autumn comes and before you know it the snow falls." Renee had grown up in various towns in Florida, Georgia, and South Carolina, everywhere snow was little more than a fantasy most winters. She'd also lived in places where the snowbanks rose to three feet overnight. "I don't want to hurry it. Travis has a few more weeks before his first official year of school." Her baby was growing up too fast. "I can wait."

Wind gusts blew down Main Street from the southwest, ruffling the pleated material of the full skirt that stopped a couple of inches past Renee's knees. She clutched the material with both hands to keep from revealing the lacy slip she wore. "Looks like rain."

"Then let's hurry."

As they passed the used bookstore, Renee's steps slowed and she peered through the window. What she wouldn't give for a full wall of built-in bookshelves. For now, her books, which included a cherished cookbook collection, were packed in boxes stacked in her bedroom closet, at least the ones she hadn't given away when her lease wasn't renewed on the mobile home she'd lived in with her husband Steve.

Val tugged on her arm. "Come on. I'm starved. If it isn't raining, we'll stop in on our way back."

Renee let her friend lead her down the sidewalk. "While we're eating, you can tell me why you were so eager for us to have lunch together today."

Val shrugged. "Can't a woman want to eat with her best friend now and then?"

Each time Val referred to Renee as her best friend—like now—a tingle of delight shivered through her.

Still, Renee couldn't help but think something other than friendship prompted Val to suggest this lunch date.

CHAPTER TWO

Renee sat across from Val at a table for four. Their waitress handed them newly printed, trifold menus. Though not fancy, the restaurant was popular during the week with those who worked downtown and shoppers on the weekend. The smell of hamburgers, onion rings, and spaghetti sauce increased Renee's appetite.

Val scanned the room. "We didn't have long to wait today. It doesn't seem as crowded as normal."

Renee's mouth watered for the richness of the cheddar potato soup, but her hair was already sticking to the back of her damp neck after the walk from the office, so she settled for a small salad and half of a BLT. Her eyes widened at the cost. "Probably because their prices have gone up. No wonder they printed new menus."

"You're right. Even though I'll answer to Pete for the expense, this lunch will be worth it." Val's voice teetered on the edge of anger.

Renee studied her companion's perfectly permed red hair and the expensive makeup covering any blemishes that dared to appear on her fair skin. Her gaze slid to the tailored silk blouse and the tips of Val's flawlessly manicured, red-polished fingernails. Val kept up with all the latest trends and name brands for herself and her whole family. She also had a husband who earned a good salary and gloated over his wife's sense of style. So, why would Pete object to Val's lunch outing? "Is everything okay?"

"Sure." Her friend's lips stretched into a smile that looked as phony as that one-word answer had sounded. "Lately, Pete has gotten on this kick about unnecessary expenses."

Unnecessary expenses. Was that her friend's problem? And wasn't that what Renee had tried to avoid over the past few years?

She peered at the prices on the menu again. Maybe this meal was a mistake. Her sandwich was in the refrigerator in the break room. What if she just ordered an iced tea and kept Val company while she ate?

Val lowered her menu. "It's only a few dollars, and we're entitled to indulge on occasion, don't you think?"

It seemed like ages since Renee had allowed herself an indulgence. For heaven's sake, this was a simple lunch, not a new wardrobe. "I suppose it won't hurt."

"Pete spends more than this at the golf course, and he goes at least twice a month when the weather is good. Shouldn't I be allowed a tiny lunch out with a friend on occasion?"

Renee knew better than to get in the middle of a couple's spat, so she pretended Val had asked a rhetorical question.

Val shut her menu. "Let's fill our tummies and have some girl time, my friend."

My friend. How Renee loved hearing those words. "All right. It's a Caesar salad and half of a BLT for me."

Their food arrived quickly, and they had almost finished when Val asked, "Is that house in Orchard Valley you've talked about still on the market?"

"I don't know. I haven't had the heart to drive through there lately." Why torture herself, knowing she couldn't live there? Not yet, anyway. "It's so pretty on the outside and has a good-sized backyard. The owners even fenced it."

Lacking a decent down payment, she couldn't buy the small, older house today. And she couldn't pray that it didn't sell until she was ready. That wouldn't be fair to the owner.

"Well, if that house sells, something else will come on the market." Val's sympathetic expression failed to comfort Renee. "God has just the right place picked out for you and Travis."

"I know." But did she really believe it, and did she have the patience to wait?

"There is one way you could own a house."

Renee lowered her fork. "What do you mean?"

"I told you. Greg Holmes is a great catch."

"Val—"

"It's been years. Put aside the widow moniker and go on the hunt for a new husband. Momma always said it's as easy to love a rich man as a poor one." Val barked a laugh devoid of humor. "I should have listened."

Yes, something was wrong in Val's household. Renee figured it was best not to push right now. When Val was ready, she would say more.

"Travis is the reason I haven't gone hunting, as you put it. His welfare is my top concern." She picked up her forked again. "Maybe when he's older and—"

"That boy needs a daddy while he's young." Val sighed. "I'm only trying to look out for you. I know how much you want to get out of that dinky place you're in."

"Well, Mr. Holmes isn't rich. If he were, he wouldn't live in the same apartment complex I'm in." Although, based on the building he lived in, she suspected his place was twice the size of hers.

The waitress passed their table with a tray of desserts. Val's eyebrows shot up. "Did you see that chocolate mousse? Let's order some."

The lunch turned rancid in Renee's stomach. "I can't."

"Oh, come on. It's only a couple of dollars."

A couple of dollars here. A couple of dollars there.

Val's voice turned sing-song. "It will make you feel better."

Renee gazed at the tray of lovely sweets. *Or worse.*

* * *

Ten minutes later, Val laid her spoon in the empty bowl coated with leftover streaks of chocolate mousse. "You don't know what you missed."

Renee grinned. "An extra two pounds?" She hadn't wanted to say no to the dessert and hoped she didn't offend Val by not partaking. "On you, it won't matter. On me, it goes right to the hips."

"Don't be silly. You're thinner than me."

Distant thunder rumbled. Renee glanced out the window. "If we're planning to stop at the bookstore, we'd better go."

If she *had* to spend money, she preferred to do it on books, but for her, the fun of visiting Once Upon a Time Used Books came more from browsing than buying.

They hurried along the sidewalk past the pharmacy, a clothing store, and an insurance office, then ducked into the bookstore. The smell alone brought Renee comfort—that musty, dusty, old paper smell.

"May I help you ladies find something?" The elderly man behind the counter peered at them over a pair of reading eyeglasses.

Renee smiled. "No, thank you. We'll just look."

"Take your time." He went back to whatever he'd been doing.

She wandered down the nearest aisle with Val following

behind her. As if of its own accord, her hand ran down the crinkled spine of a book that appeared to be at least fifty years old. The shop carried a large inventory of books others had given up because of age or space—a little like the castoffs on the Island of Misfit Toys.

She pulled another book from the shelf and gently turned the first few pages. "Look at this one, Val." She held up the book for her friend to see, then caressed the mustard-colored cover with the title in deep red. Images of a mixing bowl, spoon, and rolling pin decorated the front. "The copyright on this cookbook is 1916."

"*Mrs. Canfield's Cookery Book.* Cookery. I like that word."

"Me, too." With the book cradled in one hand, Renee carefully turned more pages as Val read over her shoulder.

Val placed a hand on Renee's, stopping her from turning another page. "Look, someone wrote a note in the margin. 'You're a talented young woman. That, along with your training, is sure to take you wherever you want to go. Never be afraid to try! Best wishes, JM.'"

"That's sweet. I wonder who the talented young woman was."

Val removed her hold on the page and backed away a step. "I want to know who JM was and his connection to the woman."

"How do you know JM is a man? Why would a man write a note in a cookbook?"

"Why not if he's sweet on the woman he's giving it to?"

Renee chuckled. "You are a hopeless romantic."

"If not simply hopeless." Val shook her head and laughed.

"Listen to this. It's from Mrs. Canfield's introduction. 'Cooking and baking are more than necessary skills for a homemaker. They can be an art form. They can be a ministry.' Isn't that encouraging?"

"Now who's the romantic?" Val backed away. "The way those recipes are written, they're antiquated today."

"And what we think of as popular in 1986 will be considered passé in another few years. Look how long eight-track tapes lasted. Now everyone buys cassettes."

"Or stays home to watch a movie on TV through a VHS tape instead of going to the theater."

Again, Renee sensed a slight bitterness in Val's comment. Pete really must be giving his wife a hard time about money.

She flipped to the back of the book. "A lot of these old cookbooks also contained household tips, words of wisdom, poems. Some were aimed at newly married women to help them in setting up their homes.

"I really like these quotations about friendship. A Sophocles quote says, 'You win the victory when you yield to friends.' And one by Henry David Thoreau says, 'Friends . . . they cherish one another's hopes. They are kind to one another's dreams.' What beautiful sentiments, especially that last one."

"I see the temptation on your face." Val propped her hands on her hips. "You love old books, cookbooks especially."

Renee closed the cover and ran her hand over it again. "Of course, I'm tempted, but where would I put it? As it is, we couldn't find Travis's shoes this morning. They're probably buried under something else I don't need." The feel of the cloth cover and the embossed lettering prompted a groan. It was only a dollar fifty. She'd saved that by not eating the chocolate mousse.

"I'm thinking of all the old-timey desserts you could make for a Cooking Capers meeting."

With a laugh, Renee held the book away from her friend. "You are temptation in the flesh."

"You won't always be in that tiny apartment. In fact, I think you'll be out sooner than you'd planned."

"What makes you say that?"

"The time is getting close."

Val was making no sense. "What time?"

"I heard that Nora Tate plans to retire next month."

Nora would quit? It was well known that her husband wanted her to join him in retirement and travel, but . . . "That would leave open the position as Mr. Holmes's personal secretary." Renee's heartbeat accelerated as she stared at her friend. "Who told you that? I haven't heard about it." And Renee worked with the woman. Val didn't.

"We have the same hairdresser, and you know how they like to carry on with their customers. Nora came in last week when I got my hair cut. I overheard them talking." Val nudged her arm. "You're great at your job. You will be a shoe-in for the secretarial position."

Her friend's compliment stoked Renee's hope. As much as she liked Nora Tate, she wanted to dance right there in the bookstore aisle.

A moment later, reality rained on her pleasure party, and she pressed the book to her body as though it could protect the most vulnerable part of her—her heart—from disappointment. "I don't know, Val. Mr. Holmes could go outside the company to hire, and Colleen is ambitious. He could consider her." Surely he wouldn't choose the prickly receptionist over her?

"I doubt it. You've been there longer than Colleen. Besides, you have seniority and more secretarial experience. Have a little faith in yourself."

She couldn't help smiling. "Thanks, Val."

"I speak the truth." Val pushed up her coat sleeve, revealing the gold watch on her wrist. "Ooh, you'd better hurry and make up your mind about that book. Lunchtime is almost over, and I want to get back to the bank before it rains."

Right. The last thing Renee needed was to be late returning from lunch. Not now. Despite Mr. Holmes's generous observation, she'd gotten to work a couple of minutes past her normal time. Not late, but later than usual.

"If *you* buy that cookbook, *I* won't be tempted, which will put me in hotter water with Pete."

Renee reread the quote about winning the victory by yielding to friends. It was like a confirmation, wasn't it? "All right. I suppose I can manage it."

In the background, the cash register dinged like a warning. Renee ignored it and carried the book to the counter. Why should she miss out on a treasure today if she would be earning more money tomorrow?

She might look for something special in the cookbook to bake for the meeting on Thursday night and prepare enough for Travis, something that would bring a smile to her son's face.

This purchase was useful, not some random because-she-wanted-it splurge. That's what she told herself as she opened her wallet and pulled out two one-dollar bills.

CHAPTER THREE

Renee opened the door to her apartment and glanced over her shoulder at her son. "I'm going to the mailbox, Travis. I'll be back in a minute. Don't let anyone in and don't leave the apartment."

Travis flipped on the television and sprawled across the couch. "I won't."

Mm-hmm. It wouldn't be the first time she had turned her back to find him standing outside or headed to the playground by himself.

With one look at the boy sitting in front of the TV, watching the *Pound Puppies* cartoon show, she shut the door behind her and turned the key, assuring herself the door was locked.

House and car keys in one hand and her mailbox key in the other, she walked across the parking lot to the covered area that sheltered the postal boxes for the apartments. She turned the mailbox key in the lock to her box, opened it, and drew out three envelopes. Setting down the other key ring in the box to shuffle through the small stack, she looked for a letter from her parents. They were stationed in Japan until her father's retirement in a few months. One bill and two pieces of junk mail. No letter. She turned to toss the junk piece in a nearby trash can and bumped into someone's arm.

Renee glanced up. *Honestly.* Would she forever prove

herself clumsy to her boss?

Mr. Holmes stepped aside. “Sorry, I wasn’t watching where I was going.”

“No, sir. My fault.”

They stood silent under the roof of the kiosk for what seemed like forever. She rarely struggled for something to say to people. But whenever she met her boss, especially in a personal setting, she either clammed up or ran off at the mouth.

She was determined to control herself this time, so she pictured herself standing with the sweet neighbor in the apartment across from hers.

“I got off lucky today.” She held up the envelopes. “Mostly junk mail.”

“Let’s hope I’m so fortunate.” Mr. Holmes opened his box and pulled out several envelopes, frowning as he sorted through them. “I guess not.”

“Have you been at the office all this time?” Oh, now she’d put on her Nosy Renee hat.

He nodded. “It’s been a rough day. I had a late meeting with the Claytons.”

His loose tie and the way the left side of his hair stuck out—like he’d run his fingers through it while driving—testified to the difficult meeting.

Even with his disheveled state, she couldn’t tear her gaze from him as she locked the mailbox and slid out the key. “Any hope?”

It wasn’t a secret around the office that the elderly Claytons grappled with keeping their greenhouse over in the next county afloat. A month ago, Renee bought an aloe vera plant she didn’t need. She’d felt sorry for them and wanted to help in whatever small way she could. Even if that meant making it harder for Mr. Holmes, who had set his sights on their land and the adjoining acreage for another development.

As the two of them walked away from the mailbox area and across the parking lot, he said, "They want to sell and I want to buy. I can't blame them for seeking security in their retirement, but they're asking more than the property is worth." He shrugged. "We're closer, so I think we'll work out something fair to both of us in the end."

"I hope so." Renee could tell through the regret in his voice that he meant what he said, but it probably bothered him that he couldn't help them by paying what they asked. She had often seen his generosity. Maybe that was why he still lived in these apartments. Maybe he was generous to a fault.

Once they reached the front corner of her apartment building, she stopped, expecting him to walk on. When he stopped, too, awkward seconds passed as they stood without moving or speaking.

Renee crushed the bill in her hand. "Well, I have a cooking club meeting this evening, so I'd better get ready for it."

"Cooking club?"

"We meet once a month to share recipes. It's mostly social, but I've brought home some delicious ideas."

"Ah. There's nothing like a good home-cooked meal."

Was that a hint?

Now, she was being silly.

He cleared his throat. "Well, I have my own plans . . . bowling with some friends."

"I haven't bowled in years." The words popped from her mouth.

"Then you're missing out."

She laughed. "The only thing I'm missing is a guaranteed chance to lose."

Glenboro had no bowling alley, but a larger town a few

miles away sported a nice one. She and Steve had gone there on a date night. Once he found out how horrible she was at the game, he wisely chose not to embarrass her again.

"I think you exaggerate. You know, maybe we could form a company team and bowl in a league." Mr. Holmes nodded as though he'd come up with a brilliant spur-of-the-moment idea. "One starts in a couple of weeks. That would be good for employee morale and teamwork, don't you think?"

A bowling league? "Do you think our morale needs improving?"

"I didn't mean to suggest things aren't running smoothly, but there's always room for improvement." He stuffed his hands in his pants pockets. "Will you ask the others if they'd be interested? We'd only need four players for each night, and I would be one. Tell them the company will pay half the cost. It will be good publicity."

"Yes, sir. I can do that."

She could see a couple of people jumping at the chance. Two others were wild cards, and Nora? Probably not. Including Mr. Holmes, that would be three probable players, one unlikely, and two maybes. What about her? Did *she* want to bowl on a league team, making a solid fourth player? Though she tried to make time in her week for social activities that let her unwind—like the cooking club, she wasn't eager to add anything else in the evenings that would take her away from Travis.

Speaking of Travis . . . "My son is alone inside. I'll see you at the office tomorrow, Mr. Holmes."

His brow crimped and his lips parted, as though he prepared to say something else, but he shut his mouth and smoothed the frown. "Goodnight."

"Goodnight."

She strode toward her apartment door, curious as to what

he had stopped himself from saying. Glancing over her shoulder, she spotted him, upper body hunched and head down in a sign of deep thought.

A bowling team? In an office of seven, could she find three employees willing to participate—four people not to include her?

Holding the mailbox key in her left hand, Renee dug into the right front pocket of her jeans for the key to the apartment door. Nothing. She patted each pocket of her jeans, front and back. No house keys. Where were they? Without them, she couldn't open the door.

Had she imagined walking out and locking it behind her? She turned the knob and pushed. The door didn't give.

Her fingers massaged her forehead as she thought back to the moment when she left the mailboxes. Surely, she had her keys in her hand. What had she—

"Is there a problem?"

She twisted to see Mr. Holmes still standing on the sidewalk. *Great.* Why wasn't he halfway back to his apartment by now?

"My apartment key is missing."

"You keep your apartment key separate from your mailbox key?"

Did he think that was odd? Foolish? Inefficient? She couldn't even say why she kept them separate, except that a house required no mailbox key. Was it her way of separating reality from the dream?

Mr. Holmes walked toward her. "You're sure you had it with you when you left the mailbox kiosk?"

"I thought so." Obviously, the keyring wasn't in her hand, so it was logical that she'd stuffed it in her pocket. She did that most of the time. But, no, not today. "It's on a keyring with . . ." She stopped herself from adding that it also held her car keys.

"It should be easy to find. It had to have disappeared

somewhere between here and the mailboxes. Come on, I'll help you search."

Renee glanced at the apartment door, shaded under the walkway that joined her building with the next one. She'd already left her son alone for several minutes. What if something happened and he couldn't figure out how to open the door?

Her chest rumbled with a subdued chuckle. How many times had Travis almost given her a heart attack by disappearing? She'd considered getting one of those plastic, child locks to put around the knob . . . still might do it.

But what if he couldn't open the door because he was incapacitated?

She pounded on the door. "Travis?" With no answer, her heart rate ratcheted up. "Travis, open the door."

"Who is it?" The small voice penetrated the wooden panel.

Renee's first inclination was to roll her eyes, but she restrained herself. After all, she'd told him to not open the door when she wasn't there. But she *was* here now. "It's Momma. Let me in, please."

"How do I know it's you? I'm not supposed to let anyone in. On TV, some people pretend to be someone they're not so the other person will open the door."

The spurt of laughter behind her brought heat to Renee's face.

"The boy has a point."

She struggled to keep from gracing Mr. Holmes with a scowl. How could she when the man was right? But with him standing there, her son's sudden guardedness was embarrassing, and the loss of her keys made her look incompetent.

Mr. Holmes stepped closer. "Why don't I try to find your missing keys while you stay here with Travis?"

Nope. This was her doing. It was her problem to handle. "I couldn't impose on your time." Renee turned her attention back to the door. "Honey, I have to run another errand. Will you be okay until I get back?"

"Yes, Momma."

Now he believed in her identity. "I'll be back in a few minutes. Finish watching your show."

"Okay."

With her ear pressed to the door, she waited to hear him move around, wishing she could see him return to the couch, but she had closed the window blinds.

She strode into the sunshine and along the sidewalk in front of her apartment, scanning the ground as she went, searching for her keys. Heavy footsteps caught up to her, providing a good view of her boss's brown leather wingtips.

She looked up. "You don't have to—"

"Renee."

That one-word, deep-voiced command hushed her, and she returned to searching the ground . . . with no luck.

Once they had backtracked to the covered mailboxes, he said, "Why don't you look on this side? I'll be sure they didn't somehow end up on the other side."

Even though she hadn't been on the other side of the kiosk, she didn't mention it. After all, stranger things had happened than to have keys up and walk away.

Renee looked everywhere, not that there was much area to search. Other than the trash can, which she inspected, everything was in the open. She caught her breath with the image that popped into her mind.

Not everything.

It was crazy, but there was one place those keys were probably hiding, the last place she recalled seeing them.

She pulled out her mailbox key, stuck it in the lock, and

prayed for success as she opened the door. "Hallelujah!"

Mr. Holmes peered around the shelter's corner. "Where did you find it?"

In her excitement, she'd forgotten she wasn't alone. After pulling the key ring from her mailbox, she held it up and jangled the metal pieces. His surprise appearance earlier must have rattled her more than she'd imagined for her to have shut the box without pulling out the keys first. "Safe and sound in my mailbox."

He grinned. "Good thinking to look inside."

But not so smart to put them in there in the first place. She locked the box, tightened her grip on each set of keys, and started back toward her apartment. "I feel like an idiot."

"Hey, don't get down on yourself. I accidentally left my sunglasses in the freezer one day. Froze a nice pair of new Ray-Bans."

"That must have been a dark time for you." She held her breath, waiting for his response to her attempt at humor.

Head tilted sideways, he eyed her as they walked. "That was cold, lady."

They both laughed. It was nice to joke and laugh again with someone whose voice was deeper than hers. It didn't mean anything, though. It couldn't. He was her employer, and she needed to remember that.

Renee stopped near the door of her apartment. "Thanks for helping me look for the keys."

"Considering I distracted you with conversation, it was the least I could do."

"I hope you have a good time at the bowling alley. Knock 'em over."

"Those pins don't stand a chance. Enjoy your meeting." He walked off, whistling as she entered the apartment.

Inside her apartment, Travis had spread his little body over the couch cushions, his focus on the TV. Relieved to know he hadn't suffered during her absence, Renee stepped to the window and peered through the blinds as her boss crossed the open yard between buildings.

"What are you looking at?"

She jerked away from the window. "Just a neighbor."

"Mr. Holmes?"

She raised a brow. "How did you know?"

"I heard you talking to him." He shrugged. "I think he's nice."

She sighed. *Yes, he is.*

CHAPTER FOUR

Renee waited on Geneva MacDonald's front porch, a paper grocery bag in her arms. In her sixties, Geneva was one of the most poised women Renee had ever met. A godly woman respected and admired by many. Renee hoped to achieve that same quality of grace and humility someday.

"Wonderful to see you. Come on in here." Geneva's soft drawl and serene voice could put even the most agitated person at ease.

Renee tightened her grasp on the bag with the ingredients for making her grandmother's Apple Slices recipe and stepped inside. She had decided to bring the dish at the last minute, not having had time to look through her new cookbook as she'd discussed with Val.

Geneva pointed to the bag. "Why don't you let me have that and I'll set it on the counter in the kitchen."

"Oh, don't bother. I'll be happy to take it myself." It would give Renee a chance to see the kitchen in this lovely ranch-style home in private. The MacDonald house wasn't large but recently built to include the latest in residential design and decor. This was Renee's first chance to admire it.

Geneva pointed to her left. "The kitchen is through that doorway in the dining room."

Renee entered the spacious country kitchen, her shoes making little noise on the soft vinyl flooring with its geometric design. Ample maple-stained cabinets lined the walls, flanked by a floral wallpaper of cream, peach, and teal. A large window over the sink revealed the backyard, a soothing view while washing dishes or preparing a meal. On the other side of the room, a breakfast area allowed for a table for six. A 16- by 20-inch framed counted cross-stitch sampler hung on a side wall above an antique sideboard. A homey, welcoming feeling enveloped her.

She placed the bag on the cream laminate counter and ran a hand over the smooth surface. Her mind conjured a similar room of her own and peopled it with those in her cooking club. In her imagination, they gathered to prepare a unique recipe. Even Travis helped. Conversation. Laughter. Friendship.

The doorbell rang, bursting her vision. She exhaled a crestfallen breath at the interruption. Well, it never hurt to dream.

Renee ventured into the den where the other five members of their club gathered, talking a mile a minute. One was Val. She started toward the couch to take a seat beside her friend, but Marie Hunter looked up and patted the dining table chair next to her. "Renee, come sit beside me."

Feeling as though she'd been called to the principal's office, she obeyed the daycare director. "I'm sorry I got Travis to daycare later than usual the other day. It was a hectic morning."

Marie chuckled. "Those things happen, and you're not obligated to bring him at a set time. Don't give it another thought. I've been meaning to tell you. Travis is a good boy, well-liked by his friends at the center."

Pride in her boy warmed Renee inside. "Thank you. I'm thrilled to hear it."

"I believe he'll be a leader. He already shows that tendency."

A leader. Popular. Successful. Everything a mother longed to hear about her child.

Val grinned. "Did Travis ever find his shoes?"

"Yes. In the bathroom cabinet of all places." Renee could laugh about it now, especially when for the past two days, he'd dressed with time to spare and she'd made it to work at the normal time.

"My daughter lost her retainer the other day. We found it in the pantry." Darlene Zimmerman, mother of three teenagers, shook her head. "Sometimes, I don't know where that girl keeps her mind these days."

"You'll find it in the same place we left ours when we were her age," said Val.

Darlene made a face. "Probably true."

Renee could relate her own story about the lost keys, but she felt foolish enough without comparing herself to a child.

After several minutes of parental commiseration, they moved their meeting to Geneva's kitchen where Renee walked the others through the steps of making her grandmother's recipe. Once the pie-like dessert had baked to a golden brown, the kitchen smelled of cinnamon and apples, and the glaze had been applied, they sat around the table to sample the result.

Shelley Armstrong closed her eyes on a sigh. "This is delicious."

Renee grinned. "Thank you. I grew up enjoying it and thought I'd share."

"I'm glad you did." Val licked the apple filling from her lips. "I thought you were bringing something from your new cookbook."

"This week has been crazy. I haven't taken the time to open it."

A few minutes later, the group cleaned the kitchen, took part in a short prayer time, and prepared to leave. Marie held up a stack of brochures in her hand. "Before we go, I wanted to make you aware of some information I've received."

She handed Renee the small brochures—thick half-sheets of blue paper folded length-wise—and asked her to take one and pass them on, just like in school. Marie was a born director. Once Renee passed them to Geneva, she glanced at the copy she'd kept for herself. Her eyes narrowed at the title. An Apple a Day Bake-off?

While the others passed the brochures around the table, Renee scanned hers. Glancing at the back page of the brochure, her attention caught on one line.

The first-place winner receives $1,500.

It went on to add prizes for second and third place, but Renee kept returning to the mention of money.

Her stomach dropped. Fifteen hundred? Could this be an answer to her prayers?

Marie stood at the head of the table. "As you know, apple harvesting season starts in a few weeks. A number of the orchards in the county have joined together to hold a contest. Of course, they want to bring attention to the industry this fall and have created a bake-off for the best recipes using local apples. I thought some of you might be interested in entering."

Geneva pointed to the second page. "It says there will be three rounds. So, three different recipes?"

"That's how I understand it. It takes place over several weeks." Marie looked around. "Is anyone interested in representing the Cooking Capers?"

Renee glanced around the room at the others, most of whom had ducked their heads as if trying to make themselves invisible. She eyed Val, who crammed the brochure into her purse, seemingly uninterested in the competition.

"Please, let's not all rush to volunteer." Marie grinned as nervous giggles answered her quip. "We only need one person to represent our talented little gathering." Her gaze slid from one woman to another until it landed on Renee, who caught her breath . . . as though that would make *her* invisible. When that brown-eyed gaze moved to the next person, Renee let out her pent-up breath.

Shelley broke the silence. "Renee brought the perfect entry tonight, don't you think?"

Uh-oh.

Five pairs of eyes centered on Renee. "But you all know how to make the dessert now—"

"Shelley is right." Val squeezed Renee's hand, hushing her. "It was fantastic, and you are one of our best bakers. Why don't you give it a shot? What do you have to lose?"

The others nodded and encouraged her to go for it.

Renee studied the brochure in her lap. Surely, the competition would be fierce. And just because she had one good apple recipe, it didn't mean she could find winners for two additional rounds. "I . . ."

I believe he'll be a leader. He already shows that tendency.

Renee had encouraged her son to participate in the kindergarten and daycare activities in preparation for first grade, to be that helper and leader teachers often sought. How could she expect him to do something she wasn't willing to do?

All those eyes remained locked on her. Marie arched a brow as though daring Renee to say no.

The thought of fifteen hundred dollars would bring her closer to her housing goal. Marie was right. She had nothing to lose but much to gain. "I'll do my best to represent the Cooking Capers Club."

As the others cheered, Renee's stomach tumbled.

Oh, boy. What have I gotten myself into, Lord?

* * *

Renee lifted the foil-wrapped plate from the passenger seat of her car, thankful that what it contained arrived at her work in the same condition as when she left home.

As she reached the outer door to the building, Mr. Holmes pulled into the parking lot and maneuvered his small Cadillac into his usual spot. Like those at church who sat in the same pew each Sunday, everyone in the office had a preferred parking space at the back of the building, and everyone knew which space belonged to Greg Holmes.

When he exited his car and looked in her direction, Renee's cheeks warmed and her pulse throbbed in her ears.

She drew in several deep breaths and released them until her heartrate slowed. She wasn't looking for a man to date, though she wasn't opposed to finding someone in the future. But a crush on Mr. Holmes would lead to nothing but trouble.

What an idiot to let Val's comments about him last week stir her imagination. She'd even dreamed about him a time or two since then.

"Good morning, Renee."

"Good morning, Mr. Holmes."

They approached the door, and he reached for the handle. "Why don't you call me Greg? Everyone else in the office does. Mr. Holmes makes me think of my grandfather."

It was true that all the other employees called him Greg. "You call your grandfather Mr. Holmes?" She could have bitten her tongue over the teasing lilt she'd added to her voice. Would he consider it a flirtation?

He laughed. "No, but others do. The man commands respect."

Like her father. "That's all I'm trying to do—show my

respect."

"Ah, well, if that's your intention, you can respect my wishes and call me Your Highness."

She raised an eyebrow at him. It couldn't hurt to be a little friendlier with the boss. "On second thought, Greg sounds less . . . lofty."

His laughter filled the back hallway as he strolled toward his office.

Enjoying the sound and satisfied that she'd shown a more personable side—within proper bounds—Renee stopped at the small kitchen and set the plate on the round table sitting in the center of the space. Her boss hadn't even commented on what she'd brought to work. Come to think of it, his focus had been on her face most of the time. What did that mean?

Nora Tate stood at the counter. She poured a cup of coffee from the commercial coffee maker, then bent over the table and inhaled. "Cinnamon. Sugar. Apples. Too rectangular and thin to be a pie, isn't it?"

"It's a little like one." Renee removed the foil and set it aside, revealing the remainder of last night's Apple Slices dessert and adding even more of its tempting aroma to the small space. She brought it to test its reception once more before deciding whether she would use it in the bake-off. Without their knowing it, her co-workers were guinea pigs.

"This is my grandmother's recipe." Would the judges in a bake-off expect something more complicated, more . . . sophisticated?

Nora studied the dessert. "Homemade crust on the bottom and top?"

"Yes." Renee grabbed a stack of paper plates from a cabinet and a knife and a few forks from a drawer.

"A glaze covering the top crust. Lovely. What's the

occasion?"

"I'm entering a contest and looking for recipes that will please the judges. Please keep that to yourself. I'd like everyone's true opinion."

Nora squeezed her arm. "I'm guessing you have a winner."

The company's bookkeeper, Debbie Norman, entered the room. She stopped at the table and sniffed the air. Her eyes closed. "Oh, I smelled something good as soon as I walked inside the building. When do I get a piece?"

Renee laughed. "Now, if you're ready."

"Of course, I'm ready." Debbie grabbed a paper plate from the stack. "Large, please. I didn't eat breakfast." Barely out of college, she looked like a walking, talking stick capable of eating the whole plateful without gaining an ounce.

Renee had cut the remaining dessert into equal-sized slices but gave Debbie two. Her heart beat double time while waiting for the woman's verdict.

"What's going on in here?"

At her boss's voice, Renee flinched. The apple slice she'd lifted for Nora fell off the knife, splatting onto the pan in a sticky, contorted mess. Was he upset that they had gathered in the break room over a snack instead of readying for the work day?

"You have to try this, Greg. It's delicious." Debbie pulled another plate from the pack and smiled at Renee, who tried to be discreet when she touched a finger to the side of her mouth, letting the young woman know a piece of the glaze stuck to the corner. Debbie's eyes widened and her tongue made quick work of the sugary topping.

He eyed the plate and sniffed. "Smells great. What is it?"

"My grandmother just called it Apple Slices."

"Looks like a flat pie covered with icing."

Leave it to a man to boil everything down to the simplest

denominator. She gave Nora an in-tact piece and served Mr. . . . Greg.

He shoved a portion of it in his mouth. Renee studied him as he closed his eyes and chewed. Once he'd swallowed, he said, "This *is* delicious. You are going to make this for us again, aren't you?"

Pleasure zipped through her. "If you'd like."

Greg's blue-gray eyes drew her in. She hadn't seen that type of red-hot gaze since her husband died. It lasted a mere moment before he looked away, leaving her to wonder if she had imagined it.

"I'll be in my office, Nora." Greg carried off the rest of his slice, almost colliding with Colleen Brewster, who stood near the doorway. "Excuse me, Colleen."

Jim Pachovsky brushed past them both to enter the room. He rubbed his hands together. "I heard a lot of talking going on in here. If there's food, I want some. Why don't you give me a plate for Dave? He's on the phone."

Renee handed him two plates with slices of the dessert and two forks. Both he and Dave were great guys to work for, but she didn't want them to think she wasn't ready to tackle her duties. "I'll be at my desk in a minute."

"Take your time." He walked out the door, moaning with pleasure.

She turned to the office receptionist, ready to fill another plate. "How about you, Colleen?"

Colleen walked to the coffee pot and pulled a cup from a shelf above it. "No, thanks. I'm on a diet."

A diet? Since when had she decided to lose weight?

With a full coffee cup in hand, Colleen left the room. Debbie let out a soft whistle as Renee stared after the receptionist. "What's eating her this morning?"

Colleen's mood had wavered up and down for the past week. But it hadn't been directed at Renee. Not until now. What had she done to cause the woman to snap at her? "I guess we're all entitled to a bad morning."

Renee thought through her interactions with Colleen recently, trying to recall anything she'd done to offend her. She came up blank. Had something happened in her personal life? She didn't know Colleen well enough to pry. If her co-worker wanted to confide in her, Renee would make herself available. Until then, she would mind her own business.

Maybe Greg was right, and there was room for office morale to improve.

Once everyone left, she grabbed a fork, then eyed what remained of the Apple Slices, recalling the two pieces she'd eaten last night and one this morning. Why risk becoming sick of one of her favorite desserts?

Renee laid down the fork and scurried to her desk. She had work to do and a boss to impress with more than her ability to bake.

CHAPTER FIVE

Music from the speakers in the dropped ceiling spread a sleepy sound throughout the office and emphasized the crawl of time. All day this Monday, Renee's co-workers had looked ready to nod off at their desks. Should she fill Nora's position, she could suggest livelier music to energize everyone.

At home and in the car, Renee preferred country music over the peaceful elevator tunes. Let her clean with the rousing fiddle in an Alabama song or mellow out with the charming twist in George Strait's "The Chair." But this . . .

She shook her head. *Bad idea. It would only distract them while they worked.*

"Is something wrong, Renee?"

She flinched at the quiet voice and turned to find Nora at her shoulder. "Not at all."

"Then you should answer your phone."

Renee glanced at the phone on her desk—at the lit button for her extension—and winced. "Sorry."

This dereliction of duty didn't bode well for a promotion, especially if Greg relied on Nora for recommendations.

She grabbed the receiver from the cradle and pushed the blinking button, then sneaked a peek at Nora as the tall, lithe woman in her sixties walked down the hall toward her office located outside of Greg's. Wouldn't it be nice to have a space with a door to block the noise that came with sitting out in the open? At least she could take comfort in knowing she wasn't stationed near the restrooms.

"Renee Burnette. May I help you?"

"Yes, you may. You can help me pick out a dress for Pete's business dinner two weeks from Friday."

Renee's shoulders relaxed at hearing her friend's voice on the other end of the line. "Thank goodness it's you, Val, and not a business call."

"What's wrong?"

"Nothing. I just . . ." She shook her head. "Never mind. Why don't you wear that pretty green silk dress you wore to your sister-in-law's wedding?"

"Mmm . . . Because I look like a tank in it." In her mind, Renee could picture Val turning up her nose at a perfectly lovely dress. "No, I want something new."

"I thought Pete asked you to watch what you spent."

"It's his function. He won't mind."

Probably not. Pete tended to encourage Val's fashion passion.

"So, how about going with me on Saturday? I'll need your opinion."

Renee bit her bottom lip. She'd vetoed the Apple Slices for the bake-off and planned to experiment with new recipes this weekend, adding a little of this and a little of that to make them her own before choosing her entry.

"I don't know, Val. It means bringing Travis along or getting a babysitter." Although her boy wouldn't mind spending time with their neighbor, the grandmotherly Mrs. Karrick, she hated to bother the woman so soon after the Culinary Capers meeting.

"Don't worry about it. Pete will be home. He'll watch the kids, including Travis. Please?"

Renee always found it hard to say no to Val, who took charge when the need arose, never shrinking from fulfilling a perceived need. Renee had certainly benefitted from her friend's compassionate works. But she could run over people with the force of a high-speed train.

On the flip side, Renee had planned to get out next week to do a little shopping. Travis needed at least one more pair of pants for school. She may as well make the trip personally worthwhile. "Okay. As long as we aren't gone long."

"Nope. I have my eye on the dress I want. Afterward, we'll get lunch."

Lunch. Shopping.

Renee smothered the groan that began in her abdomen. "Val, I have to go. I'll see you on Saturday."

* * *

Renee opened the oven door. The heat hit her face, warming her skin as though she'd sat in the sun for hours. She'd tried to be a little more creative with this recipe, so hopefully, the attempt would pay off.

Wearing oven mitts, she pulled out the pan with the Apple-Peanut Butter Crisp and set it on the stove top with a clatter.

The scent of apples, cinnamon, sugar, and peanut butter filled the small apartment and brought Travis rushing to her side. "Is it ready? Can I have some?"

She smiled down at him. "Yes, and yes. We'll let it cool first. I wouldn't want you to burn your tongue."

He groaned.

Renee tapped his nose with the tip of the oven mitt. "It won't be long." What if, for the bake-off, she paired this dessert with a scoop of homemade ice cream?

Fifteen minutes later, she spooned out small bits of the dessert into two bowls, placing both on the table. She handed Travis a spoon and kept one for herself.

He shoved a large bite into his mouth and spit a portion back into the bowl. "Ig! It's stick'n' to ma mouf."

Renee took a cautious bite and wrinkled her nose as she tried to swallow the dry oats and peanut butter. *Ick* was right. She pushed her plate away. "I was sure it would work." The combination had sounded better in her head than it tasted in her mouth. It was harder to come up with a unique recipe than she'd thought.

Travis gulped his milk, then wiped his mouth on his arm. "You'll get it next time, Momma."

"Thanks, honey bear." His confidence in her ability boosted her determination to find the perfect recipe that would see her through the first round of the bake-off. After that? She would cross that bridge if she ever came to it.

After a quick glance at the clock on the wall, Renee jumped up from her seat on the couch. For the past hour, she'd watched Saturday morning cartoons with Travis, but Val would arrive shortly. "Get your shoes on. Mrs. Sargeant is fixing to be here soon, and I need to take you across the way to Mrs. Karrick."

Although Val had promised her husband could watch Travis, Pete was called into his office for the day, which meant an unexpected babysitting charge.

A few minutes later, Renee stepped out of her neighbor's apartment at the same time Val pulled up in front of the building. Renee waved. "I'll be out in a minute."

Val climbed from the car, opened the back door, and lugged a trash bag off the back seat. "I was cleaning Daniel's closet and chest of drawers. I had no idea I'd kept so many of his outgrown clothes. I brought the best of them for Travis." She carried the bag into Renee's living room and dropped it on the couch. "You can pick through everything and keep what works."

"Oh, Val, that's sweet of you." She peeked inside the bag at the stack of shirts and pants, knowing they were all good quality. It wasn't the first time Val's generosity had helped the Burnettes. "Travis thinks your son is the next best thing to Superman. He'll be thrilled to wear something that belonged to Daniel."

Val sniffed the air. "Smells good."

"Smells are deceiving. Even Travis spit out my attempt at an apple and peanut butter crisp. And he loves apples."

"Interesting combination. What went wrong?"

"Too much peanut butter, I think."

"Can I taste it?"

"Sure."

Renee handed Val a spoon and waited as her friend scooped up some of the crisp and put it in her mouth. After a valiant attempt to swallow, her throat bobbing, Val said, "It isn't terrible."

"Yes, it is."

"A little dry." Val rinsed the spoon in the sink. "Probably a bit too much peanut butter. What if you thinned the peanut butter with a little milk?"

"That's an interesting idea." Renee grabbed her purse. "Looks like I'm headed back to the recipe drawing board."

Once they were in Val's car, Renee buckled up. "Where are we going?"

"To the mall."

She wanted to drive twenty miles away? "I told Mrs. Karrick I'd only be gone a couple of hours. Don't you want to try the boutique in town first?"

Val shook her head as she drove out of the apartment complex. "I'm sure I know what I want but need your opinion when I try it on. It shouldn't take long."

Renee's mind went back to the recipe. "You know, I probably did add too much peanut butter." Was it worth trying again? She had to be careful not to waste her grocery money on too many failures.

"You'll figure it out." Val turned onto the highway. "And if time is a problem, you can call Mrs. Karrick when we get to the restaurant."

"Restaurant?" Renee had forgotten about that part of their outing.

"Your neighbor is a gem and probably won't mind if you're a little late."

Mrs. Karrick had said to take her time. Surely, thirty minutes wouldn't matter.

* * *

Val pulled back the changing room curtain and walked out wearing a form-fitting, bright yellow party dress of shiny polyester with short, puffed sleeves and a large yellow bow on one hip. She stopped and struck a model's pose. "What do you think?"

"It's . . . it's . . ." Renee shut her mouth when flattering words failed her. How could she tell her friend it looked hideous on her?

"You don't like it."

A true friend would be honest, wouldn't she? "It isn't that I don't like the dress."

"It's the color, isn't it? I was afraid of that. My red hair clashes with it like a clanging cymbal."

"I wouldn't say it was that bad, but maybe you could try a different color. Do they have it in an emerald or blue?"

"I have dresses in those colors." Val looked down and wrinkled her nose. "I saw a red one in the catalog and fell in love with it, but this was the only one of this style left on the rack in my size."

"It is pretty."

Val turned to face the mirror in the changing room. "I want something incredible, something to make Pete proud. Are you sure I can't wear it?"

Totally sure. "Why don't we look around? You might find a dress you like better."

After a drawn-out sigh from Val and a quick change, they spent twenty minutes scouring the racks. Nothing pleased her.

Finally, she threw up her hands. "Let's try somewhere else."

They left the store and passed a noisy arcade filled with teenagers playing games on the large video machines—Mario Brothers, Donkey Kong, Pac-Man. In the background, Queen's "Another One Bites the Dust" blared over speakers, competing with the loud bleeps, bloops, and chimes that filled the space. Already, Travis asked to play the coin-operated machines when he saw them. Renee dreaded his teen years when he'd become like the boys and girls in the arcade, their full attention on the machines as they racked up points.

Val stopped at each clothing store, as well as a couple of places that didn't sell fashion items. As she tried on a dress in their final department store, Renee checked her watch and groaned. They'd been gone almost two hours and hadn't eaten lunch at the restaurant her friend wanted to try. She would need to call Mrs. Karrick soon.

Once they reached the end of the mall with nothing to show for it, Renee looked over her shoulder. "Now what?"

"Aren't you hungry? Let's hit that restaurant I mentioned."

Renee was starving. When she opened her mouth to say

she'd prefer to go home, the image of all those clothes for Travis popped into her head. Her lips snapped together. The additional babysitting charge was a small price to pay for all those outfits.

CHAPTER SIX

Val pulled into a small strip shopping center and found a parking space near the restaurant. Renee pointed to the phone booth. "I'll call Mrs. Karrick and meet you inside."

She trotted to the phone booth hanging from a metal post in the sidewalk outside a jewelry store and picked up the receiver. She inserted her money in the slot, the coins *clanking* as they dropped into the coin box, then she pushed the buttons for her neighbor's number and waited for her to pick up the phone.

"Hello?"

"Mrs. Karrick, this is Renee."

"Hello, Renee. Are you on your way back already?"

"No, ma'am. That's why I'm calling. I hate to ask, but will you watch Travis a while longer?"

"Think nothing of it. We're having a good time. That little rascal has a keen knack for beating me at all the board games we play."

Renee laughed. "Don't feel bad. He beats me, too. Thank you. I'll pick him up as soon as I can."

"You just have a good time, sugar."

She hung up, thankful for her neighbor, and joined Val inside the dim restaurant. "What looks good?"

"I've decided on the salad with grilled chicken. You order what you want. My treat."

"That isn't necessary, Val."

"Sure it is. I've taken more of your time than you'd planned. Now, get what you want."

With that, any argument ended. "I'll have the same as you."

Once they ordered, Renee relaxed as well as she could in the hard, wooden chair. Bouncy, canned music played in the background.

"I do appreciate you coming with me, Renee. You kept me from making a mistake. You were right. That color was horrible on me."

"You'll find the right dress."

When their meal arrived and Renee tasted the chicken, she moaned. "This is wonderful. They've done something special. I wonder what it is."

Val tasted hers. "I don't know."

"A hint of lime juice, maybe?"

"I think you're right."

"Speaking of recipes, how is your competition planning coming?"

"You already know how this morning's recipe worked out. I tried a couple of others, but they didn't impress me, either. I can't seem to find anything unique." She took a drink of her sweet tea. "I don't know. I might have bitten off more than I can chew. No pun intended."

Val pierced another piece of chicken with her fork. "Do you need something *new*? What about the cookbook you bought a couple of weeks ago? Was there anything in there you could improve upon?"

Renee hadn't thought to look through Mrs. Canfield's cookbook for a recipe she could modernize. "I don't know. I'll go through it when I get home. Honestly though, I don't know if I have what it takes to win a competition. I don't want to let you and the other ladies down."

"If that's what bothers you, don't worry about us."

"It's more than that, really. It's the prize money."

Val paused with her fork in the air. "Prize money?"

"The brochure Marie handed out mentioned fifteen hundred dollars."

"Fifteen—" Val wiped her mouth with the napkin. "I threw it away without reading it."

"The contest and the money won't matter if I can't come up with new ideas."

Val grew pensive and concentrated on her food.

"Hey." Renee reached across the table and touched Valerie's arm. "I know I asked once before, but is there something wrong? You've seemed a little out of sorts lately."

"I'm fine." Valerie smiled and took a sip of her iced tea. After a moment, she leaned against the back of the chair and sighed. "Things are strained at home."

"Are the kids all right?"

"Sure. *They're* fine."

But not everyone was fine. Renee ventured another question. "Is it Pete?"

Val glanced around the dining room, obviously wanting to assure herself no one could overhear, like a waitress. She lowered her voice. "We're not communicating well lately."

"I'm sorry. Is there anything I can do?"

The edges of Val's mouth tipped up into a forced smile. "No. It's just one of those rough patches couples go through. We'll work it out. But thanks."

Renee eyed Val, who returned to eating her salad. "Fair enough. But if you change your mind and need someone to talk to, I'm here."

A few minutes later, Renee walked out the door and down the sidewalk alongside Val. Her friend said, "I had no clue of the prize money for the bake-off. I suppose it makes sense as an incentive for people to enter." Val's voice took on a dreamy quality. "I can see the happy look on Pete's face if I were to win that bake-off."

Renee's lunch turned sour in her stomach. "You would consider competing?" It was one thing to compete against strangers, but something totally different to compete against a friend.

They stepped off the curb, and Val looked at her. "Would you mind?"

What did Val expect her to say? "It's open to anyone who wishes to enter."

"To be honest, Renee, the prize money is too tempting to pass up."

Renee stopped in the middle of the parking lot, her legs like lead posts. Val had a house. She had a husband with a good job to share the support of the family. For Renee, everything was on her, including the rent on that dinky apartment.

Val opened the doors of the new BMW—something. "I think it will be fun."

"Yes, but . . ." She didn't want to compete with her friend. Neither did she want to back out of the bake-off and lose any possibility of winning the prize money.

Lord, what do I do? Am I being selfish?

Or was Val the selfish one?

* * *

After fixing a quick lunch for herself and Travis on Sunday afternoon, Renee spent two hours at the dining table, searching through cookbooks for fruit recipes to modify and make her own. The competition began in less than two weeks. She needed something unique to impress the judges, or she wouldn't pass to the next round.

She pushed aside the current cookbook she was perusing. At this point, she wasn't hopeful about her chances of finding that special first recipe, much less two more should she be fortunate enough to move on in the competition.

Then there was the situation with Val. Yesterday, after stopping at the boutique in town, Val finally found a dress. Afterward, she returned Renee to the apartment, and the two of them parted as though nothing was wrong. Maybe not for Val, but Renee experienced a fitful night's sleep. Only one person could walk away with the top prize. How could they—best friends—go after the same reward and still keep their friendship intact?

She picked up *Mrs. Canfield's Cookery Book* and turned the yellowed pages. Quotations were sprinkled in with recipes. She stumbled upon two verses from Ecclesiastes that reminded her of the advantages of friendship and working together:

Two are better than one, because they have a good reward for their labor. If either of them falls down, one can help the other up. But pity anyone who falls and has no one to help them up.

A shiver trickled down Renee's spine. The scripture was true when it came to helping one another, but honestly, Renee had felt Val's announcement as a blow that knocked her to the ground. Who would help *her* rise again?

Regret rushed like a winter wind through her veins. She really was to be pitied if she believed for a minute that one little contest would prevent Val from ever picking her up—or vice versa. Over the past four years, Val had proved herself a true friend, and Renee wanted to be the same to her.

"Mom, can I go to the playground?"

She pulled another cookbook from the storage box sitting on the chair beside her and opened it to the index at the back. "It's pretty warm outside, Travis. Why don't we wait until it cools off later?"

Travis looked up from the floor, where he played with his Hot Wheels cars. "I'm bored."

So am I. "Okay. Get your shoes on, and let's go to the playground for a while."

"Yippee!" He jumped up and grabbed his shoes.

Renee slapped the book shut, deciding to take it with her. While her son played, she would continue to search for recipes. "Do you need me to tie your shoes for you?"

He gave her the stink eye. "I'm not a baby."

So he had told her more than once lately.

She sighed and grabbed her keys from the counter, then followed him out the door. At the edge of the sidewalk, she grasped his hand when he raised his foot to step off the curb. "Stop and look both ways."

Travis's head jerked from side to side. "No cars."

He pulled on her hand and they crossed the parking lot. At the other end of the apartment complex, the playground sat in shade cast by the surrounding white oak trees. Two boys swung on the swing set, competing to see who could fly the highest. A girl about her son's age slid down the slide. She had seen all the children before, knew their first names, but as usual, Renee saw no parents around to supervise.

She sat on a weathered bench under an oak and hoped she wouldn't go home with splinters. "I'll be here. Have a good time." Before she could finish getting the words out, Travis was halfway up the steps of the slide, following the little girl named Tiffany.

As she flipped pages in the cookbook, Renee kept an eye on

all four kids. They played well together until Tiffany fell off the edge of the slide. Renee jumped up, but Travis beat her to the crying girl and pulled her to her feet. In a split second, she stopped crying and smiled. "Thanks for helping me, Travis."

Bless her flirty little heart.

He smiled back. Oh, her boy would be a charmer, just like his daddy.

Two are better than one, because they have a good return for their labor: If either of them falls down, one can help the other up.

An idea glowed in Renee's brain like a neon sign at midnight. Two *were* better than one, especially when one of them felt in over her head.

After they returned to the apartment, Renee picked up the telephone receiver and punched the buttons for Val's number. When she heard the deep "Hello," she said, "Hi, Pete. This is Renee. Is Val there?"

"Sure, Renee. Hold on."

A few seconds later, she heard shuffling and whispering, then "Hey."

"Hey, Val. How did Pete like the dress?" As soon as the question popped out, Renee regretted bringing up the subject. The dress her friend bought was fifty dollars more than the one she had originally wanted, and Val had dreaded telling her husband.

"He liked it fine, even whistled when he saw it on me."

But?

"When I mentioned the price, he told me to take it back and wear the green silk."

"I'm sorry."

"Don't be. I knew what would happen before I charged it on the credit card."

"Well, if you need a babysitter that night, I'll be glad to watch the kids. I should have offered before."

"That's nice of you, but Pete's sister has already planned a great time for them. In fact, she's keeping them overnight."

"Good." Renee changed the subject to the reason for her call. "I've been thinking about the bake-off."

"Oh?"

"Why don't we enter together?"

"Together?"

"Yes. I think we could go further if we worked alongside one another to come up with the right recipes."

Val laughed. "You know, chances are neither of us will win."

"To be honest, I don't want to compete against a friend."

"I wouldn't either if I looked at it as a rivalry. It's just a matter of everyone doing her best, and then letting the judges decide their preference based on their personal tastes." Val paused. "Don't worry, Renee. We'll be fine."

Renee's stomach muscles tensed. From the sound of those last words, she had to wonder if her friend even believed what she'd said. No matter how Val glossed over the situation, it boiled down to competing against one another.

Would Renee lose her best friend when the bake-off ended?

CHAPTER SEVEN

At the end of the day on Monday, Renee slumped in her chair, too weary to pull her purse from her desk drawer and go home. Mental fatigue—not physical—held her down. She summoned the energy to turn off her Selectric typewriter and push the chair back from the desk.

"Renee, would you come in here before you leave?" That familiar, authoritative male voice called to her from down the hall.

She looked up to find Greg poking his head out of Nora's office doorway. "Yes, sir."

"Great." He disappeared, presumably, back into his office.

Renee inhaled a deep breath, hoping to calm her nerves. Had she forgotten to do something? Maybe Nora told Greg about the way she had daydreamed at her desk last week while the phone rang off the hook.

She grabbed her steno pad and a pen, hurried down the hall, and crossed Nora's empty office to the door leading into Greg's larger space.

He sat behind his desk, signing papers. "Shut the door, please, and have a seat."

Oh boy.

Moisture formed on her brow and her legs trembled as she walked across the room. Sitting in the chair across from him, she placed her steno pad in her lap, hoping all he wanted was to dictate a letter.

Greg—Renee was getting accustomed to using the informal address—continued slashing his signature on a stack of letters, not even reading them. Clearly, he trusted Nora's work. He put his pen down and looked up, his soft eyes studying her. "You're working late tonight. Rough day?"

Was anxiety visible on her face? She flashed a smile, not wanting to give him the impression she couldn't handle her job or that she didn't enjoy it. "Not at all."

He nodded. "How's Travis?"

"He's fine."

"He seems like a good kid."

"The best."

Greg settled back in his chair, hands folded over his trim stomach. "I called you in here to ask something of you."

She frowned, both curious and dreading what he would say. It popped into her mind that she'd given him the wrong impression the day they met at the mailboxes. Did he think she had flirted with him?

Get a grip, Renee.

"Nora plans to retire soon."

Renee caught her breath. Was this the news she'd waited to hear? "I know she's looked forward to traveling with her husband."

"She all but bounced on her toes telling me of her decision this morning. Her last day is the eighth of next month."

"I'm sure you'll miss her." Ugh! What a milquetoast comment.

"I don't know how I'll cope without her." Clearly, the thought worried Greg. He shook his head as though shaking away the concern. "Nora has been with me since I started the company eight years ago. I want to plan a retirement party for her. I think she deserves a proper send-off, don't you?"

"Yes, of course."

In the months she'd worked for the company, Renee had come to admire Greg's kindness and the concern he showed for others. Critics might say he ran a loose ship, but he cared about his employees and had a good mind for business. From Renee's standpoint, a major part of his success was due to happy employees who respected their boss and did their best to help the company prosper.

"I'd like you to plan it."

His request provided her with a second wind. "I'd be honored." Even as she stated it—and meant it—a pinch of disappointment dampened some of her satisfaction at knowing he trusted her with the assignment. So far, he'd said nothing about filling Nora's shoes. However, if she did a good job . . . "Do you have a time and place in mind?"

"I'll leave that to you. Look into renting a banquet space or reserving a dining room in a nice restaurant. Whatever you decide, invite the spouses and Nora's family."

She wrote his instructions on the pad and noted the excitement in his voice, like Travis's excitement whenever she gave him a dollar and trusted him to add it to the offering plate at church. "You're enjoying the idea of throwing Nora a party."

"Who doesn't like a good shindig?" He gave her a budget figure—a generous figure. "Collect the receipts and give them to me, personally. I'll see that Debbie reimburses you before the party. Will that work?"

Surely, he knew she couldn't say no.

An image of her checkbook balance popped into her head. With the extra money she was spending on recipe experimentation, she'd prefer to be given an allotment in advance, but she trusted him to see that she was reimbursed in a timely manner. She also couldn't help but wonder if this was a test. Would her success or failure at organizing the party and staying within budget determine whether he offered her Nora's position?

"That will work."

"Then keep me up to speed on your plans. I'll make the announcement of her retirement in the next couple of days, so for now, let's keep it between us."

"Yes, sir."

And what will you do about a new secretary, Greg?

He leaned back in the chair. "Has anyone committed to forming a company bowling league?"

Renee controlled her frustration at the change in topic. "Dave's excited. Jim agreed to participate as long as it doesn't interfere with a family commitment. Debbie said yes. With you, that makes four."

"And you?"

She had hoped he wouldn't ask. "To be honest, I'm hesitant to take time away from Travis in the evenings."

The pleasure on his face fell away, leaving a smile that resembled a polite reaction to a recipe gone wrong. "That's understandable. Your son needs you."

But he had hoped she would take part? *Silly, Renee.* She had probably read into that downcast expression what she hoped to see. "As long as the game doesn't run much past Travis's bedtime, it's possible I could substitute on nights you're down a player. As I mentioned before, I'm not a great bowler, but I think my son would enjoy watching the games."

Her boss's mood brightened. "Great idea. I'm no expert, either, but I'd be happy to teach him how to bowl."

Renee smiled at the enthusiasm. "He's only six."

"Is that too young?"

"Not as long as you don't expect him to throw strikes."

Greg laughed. "Gotcha. We'll have fun."

"I'm sure he'll enjoy it. Is there anything else?"

He straightened in the chair. "No. I'm sure you're eager to get your son, and I have some phone calls to make. Will you shut the door on your way out?"

"Of course."

With their business finished, Renee walked out of Greg's office and into Nora's. She shut the door behind her, then paused in the middle of the room, taking in the two plush chairs in one corner, an end table in between, the desk that was a third again the size of hers, and the potted plants set in strategic areas. It all gave the room a warm, professional feel.

Yes, she very much wanted this space for her own.

Renee's gaze skimmed the entire room once more before halting at the door. Colleen stood in the hall, peering into Nora's office. Her purse hung from her shoulder, so Renee assumed she was leaving for the day, and like Renee, later than necessary. "Goodnight, Colleen."

Rather than continue down the hall, the receptionist stepped inside the office. Her glance bounced from Greg's door to Renee. "Nice space, don't you think?"

Something in Colleen's smug look set Renee on edge. "It is."

The woman surveyed the room. "A few things will change in here soon, though."

Things will change soon? What did Colleen mean by that? Did she know Nora was leaving, or had she heard the same rumor Renee heard from Val? If so, Colleen could be fishing for confirmation of the news. Renee thought it best to ignore the comment before she let something slip.

Colleen wore a satisfied grin as if she'd accomplished what

she set out to do. "I'll see you tomorrow." She turned and walked away.

Renee stood in the room, mulling over the comment about things changing. What would give the receptionist that idea? With the recollection of that self-satisfied look on Colleen's face, Renee's fingers choked the pen in her hand. Did Colleen expect to take Nora's place?

Had Greg already chosen his next secretary?

Renee's shoulders slumped as she walked back to her desk. If so, there went a raise and her chance to breathe a little easier each month.

She laid the steno pad and pen on her desk, then left the building through the back door. Her glance shot to Greg's car, still in its normal spot. If he'd chosen Colleen to take Nora's position, why not have her plan the party?

On the way to the daycare center, questions swirled round and round in her mind. Finally, she decided she could only work with what she knew. At the moment, she knew she would remain in the little corner as secretary to Dave and Jim.

A previous thought that someone else in the Cooking Capers group take her place in the bake-off flew out the window. It was more important than ever that she win the competition.

She must win. She *would* win. Even if it meant beating Val.

* * *

Renee followed Travis into the apartment, a grocery bag in each arm. "Put my keys on the counter, please."

With a clatter, he dropped them on the laminate surface. She had to sidestep to keep from tripping over the KangaROOs he'd kicked off in the middle of the entry. "Your shoes go in the closet."

Travis opened the closet door and dropped the shoes on the floor. "Do you have to make something with apples again?"

"I'm afraid so. I told you the people who grow apples want the best recipes to help sell their fruit."

"Just don't put in any peanut butter."

Renee chuckled. "I won't." Not in this recipe.

After flipping through cookbook after cookbook on Sunday, as well as pulling out index cards from the wooden recipe box, she'd opened *Mrs. Canfield's Cookery Book* to find a promising recipe—Szarlotka—that would be the foundation for her own creation. Testing it out had required a trip to the store after work.

Hating to cut corners on supper but needing time to bake, she pulled out two cans from one of the bags. She would make a salad to go with the canned ravioli, throw a little cheese on the sauce, and hope Travis wouldn't report her for not serving him a from-scratch meal. On second thought, he would ask for seconds.

After a quick supper and clean-up, Renee ran his bathwater, opened the sofa bed, and laid out his pajamas. While he played in the bathtub, she gathered the ingredients to make what she hoped would be her entry in the first round of the bake-off this Saturday. To the basic Polish recipe—something between a pie and a cake—she would drizzle a pecan-laden praline sauce over a crumb topping.

With an ear out to monitor Travis's bath time, she placed Mrs. Canfield's open cookbook in the acrylic holder that protected the pages from her messy preparation. Afterward, she combined the ingredients for the topping in a bowl and set it in the refrigerator. She sliced unpeeled Granny Smith apples into another bowl and added lemon juice to keep them from turning brown. Finally, she stirred in cinnamon and a small amount of sugar and placed that bowl in the fridge.

"Momma, I'm ready to get out."

"Coming."

Renee dried both her son and the bathroom floor, wet and slippery from his splashing. He insisted on dressing himself before climbing into the sofa bed. "Why don't you sleep in the bedroom? I don't want to keep you up while I rattle around in the kitchen."

His grin stretched from ear to ear, prompting another round of guilt on Renee's part. Her son liked having a bedroom of his own, and she didn't blame him for his excitement.

Soon.

In the meantime, she saw in her future a night of tossing and turning on the sofa bed—uncomfortable under an adult's weight. But it would be worth it if she could win the contest and add the money to her housing fund.

While the Szarlotka baked, she relaxed on the sofa bed, watching a mystery on TV. The oven timer dinged, and she removed the dessert to the counter to cool.

A few minutes later, a knock sounded on her door. She glanced at the kitchen clock. Eight forty-seven. Who would be calling this late?

Renee peered through the door's peephole and frowned. *What on earth?*

She opened the door. "Mr. . . . Greg."

"I'm sorry to drop by so late. I had a meeting that went longer than I'd hoped."

Okay, but that didn't explain why he'd dropped by at all. "Come in."

He stepped into her apartment and stopped, his focus on the rumpled sofa bed.

Renee's face burned at having forgotten about it before inviting him inside. "I . . . um . . . I'm baking so I put Travis to bed in my room."

Greg reached into his suit coat and withdrew a rectangular piece of paper from an inside pocket. He held it out to her. "I thought about it and realized it wasn't fair of me to ask you to pay for Nora's party upfront. This should cover most of the expense. If you need more, just ask."

She took the check and glanced at the amount—the generous amount. "Thank you. That does help."

He nodded as if seeing her living arrangement convinced him that he'd done the right thing. *Poor Renee. She needs this.*

He sniffed the air. "It smells good in here. You've baked those apple slices again?"

"No. This is a different recipe, but it is made with apples."

"We're getting into the season."

Renee laughed. "Oh, I'm not baking these desserts because I love apples. I like them, all right, but I'm trying to come up with something new."

"I remember you mentioning a cooking club. I guess that means you enjoy puttering around in the kitchen."

"I do."

He eyed what she had dubbed her Queen Szarlotka cooling on the counter. Since the dessert was pronounced Shar-lot-ka, she gave it the royal title in honor of the woman for whom the city of Charlotte, North Carolina was named.

"Are you bringing it to work tomorrow?"

She smiled at the hope in his voice. "I'll taste it first to see if it's worth bringing. I added my own twist to the recipe, and my past experimentation hasn't gone well." She tilted her head. "Actually, I could use a second opinion."

Greg rubbed his hands together. "Hand me a fork and you'll get it. My taste buds are yours."

"Okay. Have a seat at the table."

Renee grabbed a knife and cut into the dessert, releasing more of the heavenly aroma. What if it smelled much better than it looked? She placed a piece of the creation on a small plate for him and did the same for herself.

After giving him his piece, she set the other plate on the opposite side of the table, where she slipped into a chair. Picking up her fork, she cut off a small portion and raised it to her lips. "Here goes nothing."

The flavors burst in her mouth. Sugar—not too sweet. Cinnamon. Tart apple slices cooked to perfection. The nutty, buttery, brown sugar sweetness of a thick praline topping, her own addition. Surely, this was it, because she had the hopeful notion God served this dish in heaven.

Renee dipped her chin and cut her eyes sideways to catch Greg's reaction. Her heart thrummed at the seriousness in his expression, the purposeful chewing and pinched eyebrows. He stopped chewing and stared at her, his silence nibbling at her patience.

Renee drew in a breath. "Well?"

"Amazing. Really amazing."

Her shoulders sank with the release of the air in her lungs. "Do you think it's good enough to enter a bake-off?"

His eyes widened. "A bake-off?"

"The first round of competition is Saturday, and I'm still not sure what I'm presenting. I'm hoping tonight's recipe will be it." She left the rest of her explanation hanging.

Greg set his fork down. "Is that the bake-off sponsored by the apple industry?"

The cautious note in his voice, piqued her curiosity. "Yes. You've heard about it?"

"The apples should have sent off a warning bell in my head." He frowned. "I'll call the committee tomorrow and take myself off the judging panel."

Renee's pleasure retreated. "You're a judge for the bake-off?" No wonder his expression had turned wary when she mentioned it.

"Supposed to be. It's clear, though, with you in the competition, I won't be unbiased." From the softness in his voice and the shy smile, Renee suspected Greg's claim had little to do with her baking.

"You don't have to bow out because of me. I'll find something else to enter."

"Don't you dare. To be honest, I'm in your debt."

"How is that?"

"I won't need to sample a slew of dishes prepared by strangers. You've saved me from having to come down with some exotic disease that would keep me from attending Saturday."

While she fumbled for a response to his lighthearted banter, he polished off the rest of the dessert. He set down his fork and glanced toward the closed bedroom door. "I'd better leave before I wake Travis. I'll see you in the morning, Renee."

She walked him to the front door. "Thanks for being my taste tester. You took your life in your hands."

"Believe me, it was my pleasure and no risk at all."

"Good night." She opened the door for him and stood there until he'd disappeared into the darkness.

Once Renee shut the door, she leaned with her back against it. She wasn't sure what surprised her most—his being a judge for the bake-off, the longing on his face when looking at her, or her disappointment in knowing he would withdraw his services for the event.

She winced as a shameful part of her had rejoiced for a moment at the advantage she imagined his participation would have given her.

CHAPTER EIGHT

Like the birthday girl blowing out her candles, Renee stood at the door of the Glenboro High School auditorium-slash-gymnasium and blew out a gusty breath until her chest ached. Unfortunately, it failed to calm her nerves.

Entering the spacious room with the Queen Szarlotka in her arms was like walking into a bakery that specialized in scrumptious apple desserts.

A large crowd of people, probably eighty to one hundred, mingled or meandered. They stood in groups or sat in open bleachers lining the hardwood floor, the wood's painted surface proving the room doubled as a basketball court during the season.

A man near the stage snapped photographs. The sizeable lens attached to the camera pegged him as a photojournalist. A female reporter stood nearby with a microphone in hand, interviewing a woman who smiled at the camera while wringing her hands. Renee recognized the call letters and channel number as belonging to an Asheville news station.

This was a bigger deal than she'd imagined.

How many people were here to compete? A good portion, based on the number of dishes covering the surfaces of three long rows of tables from the cafeteria, two tables to each row. She swallowed the groan that tickled her chest. She didn't have a chance.

A hand touched her elbow and her head jerked to find Greg at her side. "Relax, Renee. You'll do fine."

"I don't know. I never dreamed so many people would enter the competition." She'd imagined a couple of dozen. "There must be fifty or sixty desserts on those tables, and people continue to arrive." And the news coverage. She hadn't prepared herself for something like that, though she could understand the apple growers seeking the publicity.

"Maybe, but they don't have what you have." At her quizzical look, he leaned down and whispered in her ear, "A winning recipe."

Oh, that was sweet. He knew how to set her at ease.

At least, when it came to his encouragement. As far as being at ease in his presence, that was another thing altogether. She'd rarely seen him dressed in anything other than a suit and tie. Today, her heart fluttered at seeing him in a lightweight navy blazer over a blue plaid button-down shirt—open-necked and no tie, navy pleated trousers, and Top-Siders on his feet. Casual, yet classy.

Realizing she was staring, she faked a light cough and found her voice. "Thank you."

He shrugged. "I mean it."

"Did you change your mind about judging?"

"No. I handed in my resignation."

Relief swept through Renee. Not that she thought she would ever take advantage of her connection to Greg, but she'd lived long enough to realize that the moment the word "never" slipped into her mind, temptation slipped in right behind it.

And it was nice to see his integrity in action.

"You didn't tell me how you got involved in this event." She had seen little of him since Monday night, and then only when passing in the office hallway.

"I have a friend who owns an orchard. I was asked to take part."

"You had your opportunity to escape this madness. Why didn't you take it and decline?"

Greg grinned. "I came to cheer when my neighbor and employee makes Holmes Real Estate Developers proud. Maybe when the competition is done, we'll hang a banner above the front door." He waved his hand through the air as though reading what it would say. "'Workplace of Renee Burnette, winner of the 1986 An Apple a Day Bake-off.'"

Renee shook her head but couldn't stop grinning. "Nothing like a little pressure to keep the butterflies in line."

"Actually, the emcee they'd lined up called in sick, so they drafted me."

"That exotic disease you considered catching?"

His burst of laughter brought a full smile to her face. "Better him than me."

She had conversed with Greg—talked of things other than business with him—more in the past almost three weeks than she had in the previous months she'd worked for his company.

"Where's Travis?"

"He's with his grandparents this weekend. I figured this afternoon would bore a six-year-old."

"Probably." They stood in silence for a moment, then he said, "I've been so busy this week, I forgot to ask. How is the planning coming for Nora's party?"

Would he approve of the venue she'd chosen? "The Emperor Hotel downtown has a banquet space I think fits our needs. I've heard the food is good. It's a beautiful room and the hotel has given us a good price." She quoted the estimated amount for both the room and a buffet dinner for twenty-five. Once she got a firm head count, the price could go down.

"That sounds fair. I've had meetings in that room. The hotel staff has gone out of their way to be of service. Good thinking, Renee."

"I'm glad you approve. I'll book it first thing Monday." Although she wasn't sure she wanted to know the answer, she had to ask anyway. "I need to know if you'll bring someone . . . for the headcount, of course."

"Of course. No, I'll come alone. What about you?"

He hadn't missed a beat in turning the question back on her. Val's claim that Renee should consider a romance with Greg kept popping up at odd times, words she tried to forget because they prodded her into imagining such a thing, such a promising fantasy. "Just me."

His eyes flared with something she couldn't pinpoint, but when he merely nodded, she looked around, focusing on where to take the Szarlotka she still held.

As though he sensed her problem, Greg pointed to an area on the stage. "They expect you to check in. The ladies will assign you a table for your entry."

A short line of mostly women, holding as tightly to their dishes as she did, stood on the stage, waiting for their turn to sign in at a table manned by two middle-aged ladies.

As Greg accompanied her to the steps leading to the stage, Renee glanced around. "I don't see my friend. She's competing, too." Had Val decided not to enter the bake-off after all? The thought brought a sense of relief that was short-lived when Renee spotted all four members of the Sargeant family across the room. "There she is. And all the members of the Culinary Capers are here."

Greg followed her gaze. "Culinary Capers?"

"My cooking club. I mentioned it the day I—" She scolded herself for bringing up the embarrassing day she locked her keys in her mailbox. "They're all here."

"Do you want me to go over and let them know where you are?"

As he spoke, Val waved, then the others followed suit. "They've seen me." *Us. They saw us standing next to one another and there would be no end to the questions, especially from Val.*

Renee shifted the covered plate again to free a hand. Her return wave worked like a beacon, luring everyone closer.

Val beamed. "For a while, I wondered if you'd changed your mind."

Renee wouldn't admit she'd wondered the same about her friend. "Not at all." She gestured to Greg. "This is my boss, Greg Holmes. Greg these are my friends, Pete and Val Sargeant, and their children, Melissa and Daniel." She also introduced each lady from the Culinary Capers group.

The men greeted one another with handshakes, while Val looked Greg up and down. Clearly putting two and two together to get five, her sparkling gaze landed on Renee, and she winked. Renee attempted to tone down her friend's enthusiasm with a subtle shake of her head. But hadn't she let her own imagination run in that direction just minutes ago?

Greg looked at his watch. "If y'all will excuse me, things will get rolling soon, and they'll be looking for me."

Renee stepped back. "I'd better check in. I'll be back in few minutes."

Ten minutes later, she placed her dish on Table Three, laid a card with the recipe in front of it, as instructed, and rejoined all of her friends. "I don't know about you, Val, but I'm nervous."

Val squeezed her hand. "Just treat this as a fun adventure."

Renee grimaced. She could say that. She didn't have as much riding on this competition.

"You never told us your boss was such a good looking guy." Shelley batted her eyelashes and laughed.

"Or that you were such good friends," added Darlene.

Even Marie couldn't let it go. "My cousin is a waitress at Gully's. She pointed him out to me one day and said he was single and would be a good catch for someone special."

"It isn't that way at all. He's here today as the emcee for the bake-off."

"Oh, so that's why I spotted him waiting by the door and saw him pounce when you walked inside?" Val crossed her arms and raised her ginger eyebrows, daring Renee to refute her statement.

"I think you imagined the pouncing part."

The speaker system squealed, and from the stage, Greg rubbed his ear, exaggerating the motion. "If you still have your hearing after that . . ."

People chuckled and moved to the bleachers on either side of the gym. The Capers ladies found second-row seats.

"My name is Greg Holmes, and on behalf of our apple growers' association, I'd like to welcome you to the first annual An Apple a Day Bake-off. We want to thank all of our sponsors, both businesses and individuals. You'll find them listed in the pamphlets at the door and around the room. Please take one before you leave."

Val leaned sideways and, over the applause, said, "When this is over, I want to know everything."

"There's nothing to know."

"Uh-huh."

The applause died down and Greg scanned the room. "We're delighted that fifty-four of you chose to share your prized apple recipes with us. What a great start for an event that our orchard owners hope will become an annual competition. For your participation today, each of you will receive this handsome 'An Apple a Day' apron." He held up a bib apron in dark green. On the bib portion was a large apple tree with the words "An Apple a Day" printed on top, and "1986" underneath.

"Put it on!" shouted someone in the crowd.

Greg stilled, then good sport that he was, shrugged and slipped the neck strap over his head, tied the ties, and strutted back and forth along the stage, hands on his hips like a fashion model. Several people whistled, while Renee and the others erupted in laughter and applause.

Shelley clapped her hands. "Oh, he's adorable."

"Settle down, girl," said Darlene. "Remember you're a happily married woman."

"Of course, I am. I only pointed that out for Renee's sake."

Renee considered it a wise move to say nothing and hope they would take the hint.

Grinning at his own shenanigans, Greg took off the apron and handed it to one of the women on the stage. "Here's how this will work for today, the first round of the competition. Entrants were each assigned a table row for their entries—one, two, or three."

As Greg spoke, Val whispered, "I'm two. What row are you?"

"Three." Renee's focus returned to Greg.

"—row of tables has been assigned three judges, who will sample the dishes and score them according to taste, texture, and originality. Once all the dishes have been sampled and judging finished, scores will be added. The top four recipes from each row will advance to the next round of the competition."

Twelve winners. Twelve out of fifty-four. Renee's stomach twisted. One out of every four and a half. Those weren't horrible odds. But were they good odds? Everything on her table looked delicious.

"Let's get started." Greg nodded to the judges, who turned to their assigned tables.

"Good luck, Renee."

She slipped her arm through Val's. "You, too." At least they wouldn't directly compete against one another in this round.

As the judges worked, Greg remained on the stage with the microphone and read the names of the types of dishes by table. Afterward, he provided a little history of the apple business in the Glenboro area.

When the judges approached the area of the table where Renee's entry sat, she craned her neck, trying to see their reactions. The ladies and gentlemen were well-trained, providing neutral expressions after everything they tasted.

As each team of judges finished, they took their scores to the ladies on the stage. A nerve-wracking forty-five minutes after it began, the last tallies were in, and the results were handed to Greg.

"Ladies and gentlemen, our gracious judges have reached their decisions. From Row One . . ." He read off the four names of the bakers who would proceed to the next round, along with the names of their dishes.

Renee's heartbeat bruised her chest as she waited for the winners from her table.

"From Row Two, we have Mrs. Carol Rhodes with her Apple Upside Down Cake and Mrs. Valerie Sargeant for her," he paused and glanced at Renee, "for Val's Apple Slices."

Renee's stomach clenched as she reran Greg's last words through her mind.

The Sargeant children bounced up and down on the wooden bleacher seats, creating a small earthquake, and Pete kissed his wife. Val's eyes sparkled and she hugged each member of her family.

The other two finalists from the second row were lost to Renee as she gaped at her friend. "You used my grandmother's recipe?"

"I used the idea of your grandmother's recipe as a base and added my own touches." Val frowned. "I didn't think you would care since you decided not to use it yourself."

She didn't think Renee would care? What if she had changed her mind and brought the same thing? Well, that probably wouldn't have mattered to the judges, but it would have mattered to Renee, especially if her friend improved upon it in a way Renee hadn't considered. And how would she feel if Val won using the recipe and she didn't?

To be fair, Renee had given the recipe to each of the Culinary Capers members at the last meeting. And hadn't she done much the same as Val with the Szarlotka—taken the recipe and added her own touches? Probably most, if not all, the contestants had started with someone's existing recipe. It wasn't worth losing a friend over. Besides, she should be proud that a form of her grandmother's dessert won the contest for Val. "You're right. Congratulations, Val."

"And for her Queen Szarlotka, Mrs. Renee Burnett."

"Ms. Renee, you won, too!" Melissa tugged on Renee's arm in her excitement. "You and Momma both won!"

I won?

Renee's gaze swung to the stage, looking to Greg for confirmation. He grinned and nodded. She'd won! She would move on to the next round. She was one step closer to the possibility of taking home $1,500, of realizing her dream of a new house.

The urge to dance right there in the auditorium screeched to a halt. She would move on . . . alongside her best friend. How long could they compete against one another and not let it affect their relationship?

Oh, Val, why didn't you accept my offer to work together?

* * *

Renee increased the speed of her fingers on the keys, causing the metal, type-studded ball to whip back and forth in a blur. She couldn't wait for the day when individual computers, like the ones she'd seen last week at the company's attorney's office, became standard office equipment.

No more rolling paper into the typewriter, changing ribbons, or worrying about mistakes. Of course, her electric typewriter corrected the errors without much effort, so that was no big deal.

Jim leaned over her desk, creating a faint shadow that darkened the letterhead. "When do we get to taste that winning recipe I keep hearing about?"

She stopped typing the letter to the builders Dave had dictated, her fingers hovering over the keys. "You heard about the bake-off?"

"Greg made sure everyone in the office knew you'd won."

He had? A warmth spread through her, the warmth of pleasure, and a warmth she was becoming accustomed to feeling when seeing or thinking about her boss.

Yet she felt a need to set the record straight. "Actually, I haven't won yet. I just advanced to the next round with eleven other people."

"Hey, take a win wherever you find it. From the treats you've brought into the office in the past, I always knew you were a whiz in the kitchen. Congratulations, kiddo. I'm cheering for you to bring home the gold."

"Thank you. I'll do my best."

"You always do." His bushy eyebrows dipped. "We get to sample the winning recipe, don't we?"

Renee laughed. "I'll bring in the Queen Szarlotka this week."

"Can't wait to taste the queen."

He turned and proceeded down the hall toward his office, head high and back stiff in imitation of a queen's royal walk. The silliness infected Renee, and she couldn't stop laughing.

"What's so funny?" Colleen leaned against the wall, just inside the glass door that separated the reception area from the offices—from Renee's desk. She held a Styrofoam cup of coffee in her hand.

"Oh, Jim. He wants me to make the dessert I entered in the bake-off and bring it into the office."

"I heard about it. I'm not an apple person myself."

Was that the real reason she had turned down the apple slices a couple of weeks ago? She didn't like apples? Why not say so instead of talking about being on a diet? "I'm sure it could be made with a different fruit, like peaches or something."

Colleen paused, staring down the hallway toward the other offices, then she straightened. "Really? I'd like the recipe. That is, if it's not a secret."

"No secret. I'll bring it tomorrow."

"Thanks." She turned and went back to her desk.

Renee finished the letter, typed the envelope, and carried the whole stack of correspondence—one copy for each builder—into Dave's office for his signature.

That was another convenience with computers. She would only have had to type the letter once, input the addresses, and print out as many copies as needed, saving precious time in her day.

Had Greg looked into them? Renee could propose the upgrade to him.

But no. Not unless, in the future, she occupied Nora's desk rather than this heavily trafficked corner. That seemed less likely by the day since Greg had said nothing to her about replacing Nora.

Even if Renee were fortunate enough to win first prize in the bake-off, that money would only go so far. Perhaps it was time to look for a way to earn extra money each month. Or she could find a day job that paid more.

The idea of leaving Holmes Real Estate Developers put a damper on the moment, even as a little voice in her head said it might be for the best. Ever since the day she met Greg at the mailboxes, her no-office-romance resolve had begun to melt like the butter for the Szarlotka.

CHAPTER NINE

"Hey, Val." Renee wrapped the curled cord of the yellow wall phone around her index finger as she leaned back against the kitchen counter. "I called to see how Pete's event went last night. Did you have a good time?"

An unexpected silence greeted her until Val sighed. "We didn't go."

"Oh? I got the idea you were excited about your night out."

"I was, but Pete—" Val went silent again for several seconds. "Circumstances kept us from going." The rushed response sounded like an excuse.

Renee frowned. "I hope none of you are sick."

"We'll be fine. How are the preparations coming for Nora's party?"

Okay, so Val wanted to talk about something else. Renee could do that. "Now that the cat's out of the bag, everyone is excited and looking forward to sending her off with a bang."

"Has Greg mentioned anything about moving you into Nora's position?"

"No. In fact, I think Colleen believes she'll get the promotion." If she hadn't already.

"Why on earth would she believe that? Has she seen the way Greg looks at you? That woman is in for a rude awakening."

Her friend's support warmed her, but there was one thing Renee needed to correct. She peered around the wall to be sure

Travis couldn't hear and lowered her voice. "I don't know about a rude awakening, but Greg doesn't look at me in any way other than as an employee." She added conviction to her voice, but the memory of their conversation at the bake-off tempered that assurance.

"Renee, I saw it with my own two eyes. He adores you, and you have to admit, he stuck to your side both before and after the judging. If you ask me, when it comes to you, Greg Holmes has more in mind than a promotion."

He had been awfully attentive that day. But did it mean he was interested in her in a romantic sense, or had it been simply an employer trying to support his employee in a competition that could gain the company a little good publicity?

Renee couldn't deny her interest in him, but to let it go beyond her own secret infatuation took her into dangerous territory. "I don't want a promotion because Greg might like me more as a woman than a competent employee."

"He doesn't strike me as the type to promote you without thinking you're competent. Have faith in yourself and him." Val paused. "You do like him, right? I don't want to push you if you don't."

Renee grinned. "But you'll push me if I do?"

"Of course."

The grin fell away. "If you're right, what if it didn't work out—the personal relationship, I mean? My first obligation is seeing that Travis has what he needs, and I can't do that without my job."

"I think you worry too much. But I understand." A pan clattered in the background, as though Val was in the kitchen cooking. Or baking? "How is your search for a bake-off recipe coming?"

This probably wasn't the best topic for the two of them to

discuss, but Renee didn't want to be rude. "I have a couple of things in mind." Nothing she could point to as a definite entry. Although she hesitated to admit that to Val, she had to seal her lips closed to keep from asking her friend what she had chosen to bake.

"No peanut butter, I hope."

Val was definitely fishing.

"No, no peanut butter this time." It seemed Renee would never live that disaster down. "How are you coming with your search?" Okay, now, *she* was fishing.

"I've decided on a recipe. Pete and the kids raved about it, so I have high hopes."

"That's great." Had Val noticed Renee's need to force those words from her mouth, like pulling a Popsicle stick through her teeth? Before she got into unwelcome trouble, she decided she should cut the conversation short. "Well, I'd better go. I'll see you at church tomorrow?"

"We'll save you and Travis a spot. Bye."

Val had sounded upbeat about her recipe. Whereas Renee still hadn't come up with a good idea. It was time to scour the cookbooks once more.

Looking through Mrs. Canfield's book, she felt no recipe enlightenment, but the handwritten note that caught her eye the day she bought the book, caught it again.

You're a talented young woman. That, along with your training, is sure to take you wherever you want to go. Never be afraid to try!

Renee copied the inscription on a piece of notepaper and fastened it to the refrigerator door with a cross magnet Travis had made in Sunday school. Given the encouraging impact the words had on her, she could believe God put this book in her hands for this time in her life.

Hmm . . . That reminded her to do more praying about where God wanted to take her. Those prayers tended to come few and far between.

"Momma!" Her son shouted to her from the bathtub.

Prayer would need to wait. "Coming, Travis."

* * *

Renee found a seat in the row of hard plastic chairs behind the scoring table and pulled Travis onto her lap. She had agreed to bowl tonight after Jim said his wife was sick and he needed to stay home with their three kids. So far, most of the Holmes team was scoring pretty well. Watching Greg, she had a feeling he'd played down his experience and skill when speaking with her almost a month ago about forming a team. Strikes and spares—mostly the former—filled his score boxes.

She hadn't exaggerated her lack of ability, though. They were in the eighth frame of the final game, and so far, she'd bowled two spares, two gutter balls, and three frames with a total score of less than seven. The performance embarrassed her to the point she found little encouragement when Travis patted her on the hand and said, "That's okay, Momma, the others will understand."

She watched as Greg approached the lane, bowling ball in hand. He stopped a few feet from the foul line, his fingers filling the holes in the heavy ball.

"Get another strike, Mr. Greg!" Travis bounced on her lap.

The others, including those from the neighboring team, chuckled at her son's encouragement. Greg looked over his shoulder and grinned.

Renee laid a finger against Travis's lips. "Shh." She whispered in his ear, "We don't want to disturb his concentration."

Why she should hush him was a mystery. The walls trembled with balls thundering down adjacent alleys and crashing into pins while abundant cheers and groans raised the roof.

With each step forward, Greg went through the precise rhythms of lowering the ball—almost to the floor, swinging it behind him, swinging it forward, and letting it go. All the while, his focus remained on the pins at the end of the alley as if that stare was all it required to steer the ball to the exact spot for a strike. She chuckled at the idea that his eyes acted as a steering mechanism. Whatever worked.

The ball rolled at a speedy, straight clip down the shiny hardwood flooring. Renee held her breath for the few seconds it took the lead pin to wobble then topple and its companions to fall around it like dominos. Next time, she would follow his lead and go through the motions with her eyes on the head pin.

Travis bounced on her lap, clapping. "Was that a strike, Momma?"

Renee laughed. "It sure was, honey bear."

"Is it my turn?"

Greg had helped Travis to roll a child-sized ball down the lane as the team warmed up before their game. The man was so good to her son.

"Not anymore. This game is for the grownups."

He slumped in her lap, his head pressed against the side of her face. "Okay."

Greg took his seat behind the computer that tallied their scores. Of everyone, he was the most comfortable with the automatic scorer and had been voted the one to sit in the top seat. The last time Renee bowled, scores were accumulated on paper, which reminded her of how long it had been.

Colleen stared at Greg's back, then leaned forward in her seat on the other side of Dave and peered at Renee, smiling. "Your little boy is so adorable."

The compliment raised Renee's eyebrows. In the past few weeks, the young woman had been a pinch away from crossing the line into antagonism. Renee suspected the attitude had to do with Nora's retirement and the upcoming open position. It seemed she met competition everywhere she turned lately. "Thanks."

Colleen glanced at Greg's back once more and her voice rose. "I just love kids."

Renee pressed her lips closed to keep the smile at bay. She was wrong. Colleen had a crush on Greg. The humor died. If that was behind the recent animosity, why would the receptionist focus it on her? Val could be right. Greg could have feelings for her, and Colleen had noticed. All the more reason to take care around her boss.

Twenty minutes later, Dave threw the final ball. The scores were tallied, and their team came in fourth out of the six competing teams. It pained her to think her performance brought down their ranking.

"Good job, everyone." Greg shook Dave's hand. "Will you walk Colleen out? I owe Travis a couple of more turns with the ball."

"Sure thing."

Renee stretched her neck to peer at Travis—so quiet and unmoving on her lap—already knowing she'd find him asleep. "I don't think he'll be rolling any more balls down the lane tonight."

Greg stooped and eyed Travis. "I think you're right." He held out his arms. "I'll take him while you change shoes."

Although it felt odd, maybe a little too family-like, she

handed her son over to Greg and quickly changed into her loafers.

Colleen scowled, snatched her purse, and stomped away to turn in her bowling shoes at the counter. Without looking back, she walked out the door Dave held open for her. Poor woman. Renee should probably talk to Colleen at work tomorrow. She would tell her there was nothing to worry about when it came to competing for something personal with their employer.

"I'll take him now."

Greg laid a hand on Travis's back. "It's all right. I'm afraid he'll wake up." His voice rose no higher than a whisper. "Why don't you turn my shoes in with yours and we'll meet you at the door?"

Renee paused. It had been so long since she'd seen Travis in the arms of a man younger than his grandfathers. Greg held him with care, as if her son was the most fragile, precious thing in the world. The sight brought a lump to her throat.

"Renee?"

She swallowed and grabbed both pairs of shoes. "I'll be right back."

As she waited to turn in the bowling shoes, she glanced over her shoulder at Greg holding her son in the same way and with the same care as her husband used to hold him. She looked away before the sight brought on tears.

As Greg walked her to her car, Renee pulled her keys from her purse. "I'm sorry I wasn't more help tonight."

"Don't worry about it. It's all for fun."

She didn't think Dave looked at it that way. Who could miss his frown every time she finished bowling a frame? "Well, Jim will be back next week. The team will have a better chance to climb the league rankings."

After she opened the back door, Greg placed Travis in the

seat and buckled him in. The poor kid shifted but never fully woke.

Greg shut the door and opened the driver's door for her. "How is the recipe search for the bake-off coming?"

Renee laughed, but it was a pathetic sound. "About as well as my bowling."

"You'll find the right one."

"I hope so. The next round is Saturday. With Nora's party Friday night, it only gives me two more nights to come up with a winner."

"You have no idea what you'll make?"

"I found a recipe I think will work. My husband's mother used to make it. It's delicious, but she never used apples, and I haven't tried it with them yet. That's the plan for tomorrow night."

He grinned. "Well, if you need someone to sample the result, you know where to find me."

She scooted onto the seat and slid the key into the slot on the steering column. "You like to live dangerously."

"No danger. I believe in your talent."

You're a talented young woman. Now she knew how that young woman felt at reading those words. The confidence they bestowed. "Thanks. That means a lot to me."

He nodded. "I'll be at the bake-off on Saturday to hear your name called as a finalist."

Would he be there for her, or . . . "Another chance to emcee?"

"It's what happens when no one else volunteers."

"Don't sell your ability short. After all the news reports and publicity, you've become a local celebrity."

"Hardly." His hand tapped the top of the open driver's door in a nervous gesture. "Renee, I'm really glad you came tonight."

"So am I." Their eyes held for several quiet moments, then she faced forward and turned the key in the ignition. Travis stirred in the back seat, mumbling something about throwing a ball. "I'd better take him home, so he gets a proper night's sleep."

"Yeah." Greg shut the door and watched as she pulled out of the parking space.

Maybe she wouldn't speak with Colleen tomorrow, after all. How could she tell the woman her feelings for Greg were nothing to worry about when it was a lie?

CHAPTER TEN

"Can I help?" Travis stood on his tiptoes to peer at the mess Renee had spread over the kitchen. He ran a finger through the flour that dusted the surface of the counter, the same flour that dusted the green apron she had taken home from the first round of the bake-off. As soon as she finished tonight, the apron would go in the laundry basket.

"There's nothing you can do here." If she let him "help," she couldn't trust that the recipe would turn out as well as she'd like. After all, this was her last night, her last chance to prepare for Round Two of the bake-off on Saturday, and she hadn't settled on a recipe to enter. Last night's attempt proved tasty but mediocre, nothing she believed would move her to the final round.

"But I want to help."

"Honey, I told you—" She frowned at the little hand about to grab the box holding the phyllo dough. "Please don't touch with your dirty fingers. Why don't you practice your letters?" He took pride in his ability to write his ABCs and spell the simple words she had taught him. "You want to show your first-grade teacher how smart you are, right?"

"I guess." He dragged a pencil and piece of paper to the table and scooted onto a chair. Grasping the pencil in his left hand, he bent over the paper, intent on writing precise letters.

Renee whisked the custard mixture in the saucepan until it

thickened, then she moved the pan from the burner, ready for the next step in the recipe, unrolling the phyllo dough.

"I wish you weren't in that dumb old contest."

Renee spread a layer of the papery-thin dough over a large rectangular pan. "You do? Why?"

"'Cause I'm sick of apples."

She drizzled butter over the top of the first layer and laid another one down, repeating the step with the butter. "I understand. Unfortunately, according to the rules, apples need to be an ingredient in each recipe. But, hey, we're getting to taste new things, right? This is a Greek dessert from your Grandma Burnette, whose mother was Greek, so it's a family recipe." *Sort of.* She placed the fifth and final layer of phyllo dough on the others, adding the butter. Afterward, she reached for the Red Delicious apple slices. "I think you'll really like this one."

"Not if you put apples in it."

Renee's hand halted, her patience as thin as the dough. "Travis, I told you I have to use them in whatever I make." Not that the recipe originally called for apples, but she thought it would make a nice touch. She'd find out in a few hours, once it baked and cooled. "Winning the contest is as much for your sake as mine, so I won't argue with you about it."

He dropped the pencil on the table and shoved the paper away in a fit of temper. "Apples stink!"

Clenching her teeth, Renee placed the slices over the dough. "Go to your—" she shook her head "—my room."

More and more often lately, she had lost her temper with her son. If she wasn't careful, she might see her life crumbling easier than baked phyllo dough.

* * *

"I shouldn't have another one this late in the day. I don't want to ruin my appetite for the dinner you've planned at the party tonight. But you have outdone yourself again, Renee." Nora stood in the center of the break room and licked her rosy lips. "The custard is delicious. What did you call this dish?"

"Apple Bougatsa. Except for the apples, it's my mother-in-law's recipe. I'll prepare it for the bake-off tomorrow." Last night, after tasting one of the custard-filled bars, Renee knew she'd found her entry for Saturday. Nora's reaction confirmed it.

"I hope tonight's event won't interfere with your baking."

"No. The judging won't be until the afternoon. I'll have time to make it in the morning."

"Good. I think the apples add a hint of a tart flavor, though not too tart. They counteract the sweetness of the rest of the ingredients."

Just what Renee had set out to achieve. "I'm glad you think so."

Nora set her fork in the sink and threw away the empty paper plate. "Thank you for bringing this in today. With all you've done for the party tonight, you didn't need the added work."

"Everything has been a pleasure for me."

Nora's comment reminded Renee to call the hotel again and check to be certain there were no last-minute problems. Then, she'd call the florist to ensure the centerpieces for the tables were ready to be delivered at four. What else? She would consult her written list once she returned to her desk.

"We'll miss you around here. It won't be the same." The closer it came to the time for Nora's departure, the more Renee realized the truth in her words. Even though she often felt a tad intimidated around her—professionally—Nora was a sweet woman who had gone out of her way to make Renee feel comfortable from her first day working in the office.

Nora's grin sagged. "I'm happy to be joining my husband in retirement. We'll finally get in the traveling we've talked about doing. But I'll miss seeing all of you each day."

"Then make it a habit to drop in now and then."

"I'll do that. I'll want to know how everyone is getting along." She glanced at her watch. "I'd better go back to my desk. Greg and I have an appointment soon. It's a strange feeling to interview my possible replacement."

Renee froze in the middle of covering the dessert with aluminum foil. "Someone is coming to interview for your job?"

"Yes. According to the employment agency, she's highly qualified."

Highly qualified. Renee's stomach dropped. For some reason, this news hit her harder than when she thought Colleen might slip into the position. Probably because she hadn't believed Colleen was *highly qualified* for it.

Nora squeezed Renee's arm and disappeared out the break room door.

Pulling out a chair, Renee sank onto the seat and rested her elbow on the table, face on her palm. Greg planned to go outside the company to hire. Why couldn't he have given her a chance?

So now what?

Never be afraid to try!

She bolted upright when the words she'd read in the cookbook came back to her. Why was she sitting here like a limp little worm with no backbone? How was Greg to know she wanted Nora's job if she didn't tell him? No wonder he went outside the company to seek prospects.

Her father, Colonel Simpson, had always told her to speak up when she wanted something. He said no one could read her mind, and if she didn't make her wishes known, she didn't deserve to receive whatever it was she hoped to get. Of course, Daddy never meant for her to speak up to him, so she'd developed a habit of holding back her emotions and wishes with him. And anyone else in authority, it seemed.

She jumped up from the chair and marched back to her desk. No longer. Tonight, after the party, she would find a way to bring up the subject to Greg. She imagined herself coming straight out and saying, "Greg, I'd like you to consider me as your next secretary. I'm reliable, fully capable, and ready to start immediately."

Besides, it was becoming more and more clear that he liked her. That could work to her advantage, right? Her stomach twisted with guilt over something she hadn't even done. No way could she use whatever feelings he might have for her to get something she wanted.

A few minutes later, Nora escorted a woman who looked to be in her mid-thirties past Renee's little corner. Long blonde hair, curvy figure, and well-formed cheekbones in a gorgeous face.

Renee's chin dropped to her chest. She didn't stand a chance against a dead-ringer for Farrah Fawcett.

Maybe she *should* become a little friendlier with Greg.

* * *

Renee entered the Emperor Hotel and paused in the lobby to soak up the atmosphere.

Built in the 1890s, the building occupied half of a block on the north edge of downtown. After being sold three years ago, the new owners renovated and expanded the hotel by incorporating the adjacent building. Today, it reflected the warmth of its history through an ample display of oak trim and woodwork and a large stone fireplace that occupied a portion of the left wall.

At the same time, the lobby boasted a touch of modernity through its décor. Armchairs covered in a deep rose flower-pattern print on a pastel aqua background matched a sofa and love seat flanked by honey oak tables. Prints on the walls exhibited the beauty of the mountains. Colorful pots of indoor plants—Ficus trees, Schefflera, philodendron, and pothos—were artfully arranged to bring a sense of calm and well-being to guests.

"May I help you, ma'am?" The gentleman behind the check-in counter smiled at Renee.

"Yes. I'm here for the Tate party in the Hickory Room. I know I'm early, but I want to be sure things are ready."

He consulted a book on the counter in front of him. "That's reserved for six-thirty. I'm sure everything is in order. Let me call someone to show you the way."

Two minutes later, Renee followed a young woman in a black skirt and white blouse. They walked to a room at the end of a long, carpeted hallway. Outside the door stood a brass easel holding the sixteen-by-twenty-inch poster Renee had ordered with the sparkly, gold-lettered words *Celebrating Nora Tate as She Embarks on a New Journey.* A dozen gold and white balloons hovered over each side of the easel. Later, she would urge all the guests to sign the poster as a remembrance for Nora of this night.

The hotel employee opened the door and gestured for Renee to step inside first. It was the smallest banquet room, but perfect for their needs. Rectangular tables were arranged in a U-shape in the center of the room, with nine chairs along each side and two at the head table for Nora and her husband. Starched, white linen tablecloths draped to the floor and were topped by china place settings, heavy silver utensils, crystal goblets, and the small floral arrangements of pink and blush roses and English ivy Renee had ordered. Everything was just as she'd imagined.

"This is beautiful."

The young woman folded her hands in front of her. "I'm glad you're pleased. The kitchen staff will serve the food at seven o'clock." She pointed to another long, rectangular table with pleated skirting at the far end of the room. Several silver stands and warmers for chafing dishes stood ready to receive the baked chicken entrée and various side dishes she'd chosen. Renee had elected to have the food served buffet-style, so the occasion came across as elegant, but not too stuffy and formal.

"This is perfect."

"Thank you. I'll check in with you on occasion. In the meantime, if there is anything else you need, my name is Brenda. Just let the front desk know."

"I will. Thank you, Brenda." Before the woman took more than a few steps, Renee spun. "Wait. I have a cake in my car." She had asked Nora's husband for his wife's favorite cake, and thanks to Greg allowing her to go home early in the afternoon, she had saved him a little money by baking the red velvet sheet cake for their dessert herself.

"I'll be glad to take it to the kitchen for you."

"Let me get it."

Renee hurried to the car and met Brenda in the lobby, giving the woman the cake before she walked back to the Hickory Room. She set her purse on the seat of an upholstered dining chair at the end of one of the long set of tables and checked her watch. It was six-ten. People should begin arriving around six thirty.

About ten minutes later, the door opened and Greg walked in, wearing a black blazer and white dress shirt, but no tie. "I thought I saw your car out front. How long have you been here?"

She crossed the room, meeting him halfway. "About twenty-five minutes. I wanted to be sure everything was ready."

"Nice touch with the easel and poster outside." He looked around. "I picked the right person for this job. You've done great."

"Thank you. I hope the food lives up to the impressive décor in the room."

"Based on my experience, it will." Greg planted his hands on his hips and surveyed the space again, nodding. "Nora will enjoy this evening."

Renee bit her lip. Was this a good time to show her friendlier side? They were alone, surrounded by lovely furnishings. She would start by feeling him out about his plans. "How was your interview?"

He frowned and cocked his head as though not understanding, then he shook his head. "You mean with Miss August?"

"Miss . . .?" Renee almost choked on a spurt of laughter at the sour expression on Greg's face. "Are you saying you're not looking for a pin-up model?"

"Not even if she takes shorthand at 120 words per minute."

She gasped. "One hundred twenty?" She managed around ninety on a normal day, maybe one-ten on her best days.

"I'm sure she's an excellent secretary, but the constant batting of the eyes, sly smile, and come-hither look made me uncomfortable. I don't need that kind of trouble in the office."

Renee's face warmed at the idea of the woman flirting with Greg. Or maybe it warmed due to her own recent thoughts, thoughts he'd just made clear he wouldn't appreciate. Thank goodness she hadn't tried to flirt with him herself. "Of course not."

This was why she hadn't wanted to entertain the notion of his interest in her—and vice versa—in the first place. Office romances were poison to a working relationship. His comment cemented her belief that she should stop imagining things when it came to Greg Holmes and concentrate solely on gaining a promotion based on her ability.

Professionalism only, Renee. "Are there—"

Laughter followed Nora and her husband inside the banquet room, halting Renee's wish to ask Greg if he had any other interviews lined up and if he might consider her as Nora's replacement.

When Nora's questioning gaze shifted between them, Renee plastered a happy smile on her face. "You look wonderful." And she did, more relaxed than ever.

"Thank you, sweetheart." Nora scanned the room, her eyes bright with threatening tears. "I can't believe you did all this for me."

She tugged her husband forward. "I'd like you to meet Gerry. Honey, this is Renee Burnette. She's the one who bakes those luscious desserts and arranged everything for this evening."

Gerry's round cheeks grew even rounder. "Thanks for all you've done. My wife has looked forward to tonight."

"I'm glad." Renee gestured to the tables. "The head table is reserved for the guest of honor and her husband. I'm sure everyone else will arrive soon."

A door at the back opened and servers began bringing in drinks—two coffee urns with both regular and decaffeinated, and pitchers of iced tea, sweet and unsweetened, as well as water.

Within minutes, everyone had arrived, including Nora's three children and five grandchildren. They surrounded Nora and her husband.

Greg greeted his employees and their spouses and dates but

worked his way back to Renee. “Are you ready for tomorrow?”

“The bake-off? Yes, I think so.” Knowing Greg was interviewing for secretaries from outside the office made it imperative that she move on in the competition.

“I’ll be there to cheer you on.”

Renee’s head bobbed, but she tamped down the jump in her heart rate by reminding herself that he considered it his duty to help by emceeing in the event.

All the guests prepared to stake out their seats for dinner, but Greg raised his hands. “If you don’t mind, before we get started, I’d like to ask a blessing on our food.” Once everyone stilled, including those preparing the food table and pouring drinks, he bowed his head. “Lord, You have blessed all of us with Nora’s friendship and proficiency. We’ll miss seeing her each day, but I believe You have great things in store for her in the coming years.”

How nice to have a boss who believed in prayer and wasn’t afraid to show it.

As he went on, Renee’s throat tightened. Just last night, she had read in *Mrs. Canfield’s Cookery Book* a verse from Acts printed at the bottom of a bread recipe.

And they continued steadfastly in the apostles’ doctrine and fellowship, and in breaking of bread, and in prayers.

When was the last time she steadfastly prayed for her future, rather than saying a quick plea for help after she became desperate? Oh, she would intend to pray, but time always seemed to slip away from her.

Why had she stopped depending on God to guide her daily actions and meet her needs? She had taken everything onto her own shoulders, thinking she had the sole responsibility for providing for herself and her son.

As a shy only child whose family never settled in one place

for long and whose mother worked full time wherever they landed in the United States, it had been up to Renee to entertain herself, to fix her own after-school snacks, to do her homework alone.

Then Steve's death forced her to double down in taking full responsibility for her life and Travis's welfare. She'd become so wrapped up in thinking she must do everything herself that she'd pushed aside her trust in others.

That meant not trusting in Val's friendship or Greg's feelings toward her—romantically or as an employee.

Lately, it meant not even trusting in God's provision. The answer to her questions slashed Renee like a lightsaber.

CHAPTER ELEVEN

Renee and Travis entered the high school auditorium. As before, she stopped inside the doorway and scanned the large room. Voices of other participants, their friends and families, and a couple of reporters echoed in the large space. The next round would be even smaller, and the four finalists would prepare their dishes on-site in the school's cafeteria kitchen. But Renee had no doubt the event would be just as exciting and energetic.

The basket with the plate of Apple Bougatsa dangled from one hand, while Renee held tight to Travis with the other. She looked for Val, finally spotting the familiar red hair of her friend on the other side of the auditorium, practically in the same location Val and her family had stood last time. Renee craned her neck to better search for the second person she wanted to see.

"Whatcha lookin' for, Momma?"

She smiled at her son. When he'd asked to come with her today, she promptly agreed. She had left him out of her activities too often lately. With his exuberant "Yay!" and excited hug, she felt as though she'd already won this round of the bake-off.

No way, though, would she admit to him that she'd sought out her boss. "Let's take this to the stage, and then we'll go see Mrs. Sargeant, okay?"

"Okay."

Halfway to the stage steps, Travis tugged on her arm and pointed to the opposite end of the platform. "There's Mr. Greg."

Her son's voice carried, even over the conversations of others, or so it seemed to Renee. From his position near the back of the stage, Greg turned his head and looked straight at them. The pleasure on his face sent the wings of frantic hummingbirds fluttering inside her stomach.

He met them at the steps and reached down for the basket. "I'll get that for you. One of my jobs is to take possession of the good stuff as it comes in."

She handed over the basket with her *good stuff.*

"Hey, Mr. Greg."

"Hey, Travis. Did you come to cheer for your mother?"

"Yeah! What she made is good, and she's gonna win. I know it."

Greg held up an open hand for Travis to slap. Renee's son put his entire six-year-old power behind the high-five. Greg feigned a wince, then blew on his hand. "You're strong."

"I know." Travis giggled.

Still holding Travis's hand, Renee climbed the three steps and followed Greg to the registry table. Once she signed her name on the sheet, the gray-haired woman seated on the other side pointed to the large rectangular table on the stage a few feet away. She consulted the form. "Your Apple Bougatsa goes on that table over there."

"Thank you."

Greg had placed the basket alongside eight other entries lined up on the tabletop. Only three more to arrive. She reached into the basket and pulled out the platter with the dessert, set it on the table beside the recipe, and picked up the basket. Hanging the handle over her arm, she turned.

Greg's sparkling blue-gray gaze landed on her. "I wondered if you'd make it in time."

"I baked my entry fresh and wanted it to stay somewhat

warm, so I tried to get here closer to the start of the judging. Looks like I'm not the last to arrive."

"I heard one of the entrants bowed out, so there will be eleven of you competing this afternoon."

Nine strangers and a good friend. "That's a shame." Although it meant better odds for her, Renee wouldn't celebrate over an illness or whatever caused the person to stay home.

"Nora brought me a piece of your . . ."

"Bougatsa."

"That's it. She brought me a piece yesterday." Greg whistled his approval. "I have a weakness for a good custard filling."

"I'm hoping the judges also have a weakness for custard." She prayed for it.

"Nora called me this morning to let me know again that she and her family had a great time last night." He laughed. "Around the office, she's always the consummate professional, serious and hardworking. Seeing her flitting around the room like a social butterfly, chattering and laughing, was strange. I didn't realize how ready she was to leave us."

"She's ready for a new stage in her life, like breaking out of the cocoon to become that butterfly."

"I guess." He gestured with a tip of his head toward the other side of the room. "Your friends are over there."

"I saw. We plan to watch the judging with them."

"Then I'll let you join them. I'm supposed to get started soon, anyway. Before you go, though . . ." He inhaled a deep breath as if he needed the lungful of air to finish his sentence. "After the judging is over, I thought maybe you and Travis would like to stop by Gully's with me for some ice cream . . . if you have time." He rushed on. "My treat. Consider it a celebration of sorts."

Renee's jaw slipped, and she stared at him. Why would he

want to take them for ice cream? "Uh . . ."

"Even if you don't advance—which I think you will," he hurriedly added, "consider it a thank you for all your hard work in putting together Nora's party."

"That was part of my job." And a task she had hoped would show her qualified to be his secretary.

Travis tugged on her hand, breaking the spell that had her thinking she and Greg stood alone in the room. "Can we, Momma? I want ice cream."

"Gully's serves some delicious butter pecan." Greg's dark eyebrows waggled like Tom Selleck's on *Magnum P.I.* Her boss was every bit as appealing as the actor.

"It isn't necessary to take us out." Did that sound too much like she thought it was date? Or did it sound like she wasn't interested in a date? "But I don't want to disappoint anyone, so—"

"Yippee! Ice cream!"

Greg laughed at her son's enthusiasm. "I think you made the right decision."

* * *

As they sat in folding chairs in front of the stage, Val alternated between tapping a red-polished nail against her tooth and chewing on it. "This is torture."

Renee smiled, even though her nervous stomach agreed. "I know. Every time a judge scoops up a small spoonful, I want to run from the room, screaming." They would taste the dish, then rinse their mouths with water to prepare to sample the next entry. The judges moved on in a casual manner, as though the competitors weren't watching, muscles tense and breath held.

Marie, sitting with Travis on her lap, reached out and patted

Renee's hand. "Whatever happens, you two can walk away with the knowledge that you did your best. As far as we're concerned, you're both winners simply by showing the courage to enter."

Darlene and Shelley, seated on the other side of Val, agreed with encouraging nods. Renee missed Geneva, though. She hadn't been able to attend today's event. How would the older woman respond to the waiting? With calm, cool, and patient poise, of course. Renee had tried to emulate Geneva's composure. So far, it wasn't working.

She searched the facial expressions of the judges when each sampled her Bougatsa, but they were excellent actors, not giving anything away. If she were fortunate enough to move on, how would she ever survive the final round—baking on-site without the option of starting over if she made a mistake, and waiting for the judges to declare the name of the top prize winner?

Val tilted her head until her hair touched Renee's. She kept her eyes on the stage as she whispered, "At least, you've already received good news."

"I have? What?"

"I saw earlier that you and Mr. Dreamboat were making progress in your relationship."

Renee drew back and gaped at her friend. "Oh no, Val. That isn't how things are at all. In fact, last night he told me he doesn't—and I quote—need that kind of trouble in the office."

Val gasped. "You let him know you were interested, and he said that to you?"

While Renee found comfort in her friend's outrage, she couldn't let her think ill of Greg. "No, he was talking about something that happened during an interview. He's too nice to say something like that to someone's face. He's a good man and a good boss, but there is nothing personal to our relationship."

"Really? I guess Monday morning I should make an

appointment to get my eyes checked." Val chuckled. "What I saw meant nothing but trouble . . . of the romantic kind."

"Greg Holmes is only interested in my ability to type and take dictation, and he doesn't seem too interested in that." Renee recognized the whine in her voice.

Val rolled her eyes before turning her focus back to the stage.

Travis shifted in the chair next to Renee, reminding her that, even though they had kept their voices low, he probably heard. How much had he understood of their conversation?

Eager to change the subject, she asked, "Where are Pete and the kids?"

"Melissa had gymnastics and Daniel has a soccer game in a few minutes." Val checked her watch. "I wish those judges would hurry, so I don't miss seeing him score a goal."

"I want 'em to hurry, too, 'cause I want ice cream."

Renee's breath caught at Travis's statement. The last thing she desired was for Val to know Greg had asked to take them for ice cream after they left here. Her attempt at a laugh sounded sick in her ears. "Well, we don't want them to rush through it and give any old score."

"True. I already have a recipe planned for the final round."

"You do?" Renee hadn't settled on her recipe for this round until two days ago. She had no idea what she would do if she advanced to the final round.

Val's eyes widened. "You haven't picked a dish yet?"

"I figured I'd wait to see if I moved on." Renee wished to kick herself. She should have planned better.

"When are they gonna get done, Momma?" Travis slumped in Marie's lap and folded his arms in front of him. "I'm bored."

"Soon, honey bear. Hang on."

A few minutes later, the scores were handed to the woman who had registered Renee's entry. She tallied the numbers on a calculator and double-checked the totals printed on the paper roll against the three sheets from the judges. Once she'd written on a four-by-six index card, she handed it to Greg.

He stepped to the edge of the stage. "Ladies and gentlemen, we have our four bakers for the third and final round of the bake-off coming up in three weeks."

Renee tensed. Even Greg kept a neutral expression, looking out over the audience rather than at one person. He certainly didn't look at her. Oddly, she breathed easier. She wasn't sure she could go through this again. But thinking of that tiny apartment reinforced her determination to see it through . . . if she were given the opportunity.

"Here are your final four contestants in no particular order. Betty Allen."

Everyone applauded.

"Wendy Sellers."

More applause.

"Valerie Sargeant."

Renee clapped with enthusiasm and congratulated Val, though inside, she wanted to cry. If her name wasn't the last name called, she would support her friend.

She could.

"And the last baker is . . ." Greg paused for effect. "Renee Burnette."

Ugh! There went her hopes for a house, up in sm—

Wait.

She tented her hands in front of her mouth. Did he just call her name? She sat forward in her seat, staring at him. That glorious smile and a subtle nod assured her she had heard him right.

"The apple industry sponsors want you to know that you are all winners in their book, and we thank you for your efforts in support of this year's An Apple a Day Bake-off. We hope you'll participate again next year." He reached down and picked up a large grapevine basket. "Each of today's participants will go home with one of these baskets filled with apple-related kitchen accessories. Congratulations, ladies."

Applause filled the room. When it died, people rose from their seats and filed out of the double doors of the auditorium, leaving a few stragglers and all the Culinary Capers ladies.

"Did you win, Momma?"

"I have another chance to win, Travis. Isn't that exciting?"

He shrugged his shoulders. "I guess."

She frowned at the lack of enthusiasm in his voice. "What's wrong?"

"More apples!" He poked his tongue out and pretended to gag.

Val laughed. "I think he's trying to tell you something."

"Like I should back out of the final round? Well, I haven't come this far to give up now." Renee's sharp voice carried in the growing quiet of the building.

Val studied Renee with eyes that first expressed disbelief, then turned cool. "I have a soccer game to get to." She gathered her things and walked away.

Renee closed her eyes and rubbed her forehead. Why had she let her insecurity cause her to become confrontational and rude? "Val . . ."

Her best friend disappeared through the auditorium door. Each of the cooking club members muttered a goodbye or squeezed her arm as they left.

She couldn't look any of them in the eye.

CHAPTER TWELVE

Greg held open the door to Gully's for Renee and Travis to enter. Cool air blew over Renee's skin, bringing to mind the coolness in Val's eyes after Renee's outburst in the auditorium. What had gotten into her? She owed her friend a groveling apology.

The place held a smattering of people, not nearly as many as would be here for supper in a couple of hours. Greg pointed to a side wall. "There's a table over there."

With her hands on Travis's shoulders, Renee guided him to the Formica-topped table and he scooted onto the black padded seat of a metal chair against the wall.

Greg pulled out the chair next to Travis for her, the glides on the legs *shushing* along the linoleum floor. She offered him an appreciative smile while trying not to read more into his attention today than necessary. "Thanks."

As soon as Greg slipped into a chair across the table from them, a waitress appeared with glasses of water and menus. "What can I get y'all today, Mr. Holmes?"

"We came in for some of your homemade ice cream, Jeanie." He looked at Travis. "Do you know what you want?"

Travis nodded. "Chocolate with whipped cream and a cherry."

Renee caught the waitress's eye. "A child's-sized scoop of the ice cream for him, please. No toppings."

"But, Mom—"

"You've had plenty of sweets lately." She smiled at the waitress. "Just the chocolate ice cream."

Travis scowled. "Yes, ma'am."

"What about you, Renee?"

She glanced at Greg. "You said the butter pecan is good?"

"The best."

She turned to the waitress. "I'll have a scoop of that."

Renee had wanted to order iced tea, unsweetened, after taste-testing so many desserts lately. She felt every calorie when she zipped up her pants. But it seemed important to Greg that she and Travis share in the Gully's ice cream experience.

He gave Jeanie back the menus. "I'll have two scoops of your butter pecan."

When the woman left, Renee leaned forward. "You must eat here regularly." A twinge of jealousy had overcome Renee when Greg smiled at the good-looking waitress and she smiled back. What was wrong with her emotions this afternoon?

"Probably two to three times per week. I don't cook, so it's either sandwiches at home or restaurant fare." He sipped his water. "Have you always enjoyed cooking?"

"Daddy was in the military and Momma worked, so I learned to make meals at an early age. I found I liked experimenting with various ingredients to see how they would turn out." She laughed. "Early on, sometimes, it worked. Sometimes, supper went straight into the trash can."

"Well, you've proved your ability these last weeks."

"I've tried." And in the process might have lost a friend.

They sat in near silence until Jeanie the Waitress brought the ice cream. Renee sampled the butter pecan and moaned with pleasure. "You were right. This is fantastic."

Between spoonfuls of the treat, they talked about various subjects of interest to all of them—bowling, favorite foods,

Travis's upcoming venture into first grade. Renee melted like the ice cream over the way Greg included her son in the conversation.

Travis told jokes he'd heard at daycare, the kind that most people would roll their eyes at hearing. Greg laughed at each one as though they came from a Saturday Night Live skit.

He scooped up a dollop of the butter pecan treat. "So, Travis, what do you think of your mom getting to go to the next round of the bake-off?"

"I wish it was over and she didn't have to do it no more." He shoved a spoonful of the chocolate ice cream into his mouth.

"Travis." Renee sent a sheepish glance Greg's way. "He's tired of eating apples."

The boy swallowed. "I don't like the smell of them anymore either."

She shrugged. "I can't say I blame him. I'm getting a little tired of them myself."

Greg gave her an encouraging grin. "It's only one more round."

"The problem isn't the rounds. It's the search for the right recipe. I have to test various ones to see which might be worth entering." Her wry chuckle sounded hollow. "I'm sure by now the smell of cooking apples has penetrated the apartment walls and my neighbors are circulating a petition to have me evicted. Which, come to think about it, is ironic."

"Why's that?"

"My whole purpose in entering the bake-off was to win the prize money to add as a downpayment on a house."

"You're buying a house?"

"Not yet. I'm saving for it. I know it's a longshot, but winning first prize in the bake-off would get me closer to what I need." *As well as you hiring me as your executive secretary.*

"Will I get my own room, Momma?"

She smiled at her son. "Yes, you will. Isn't that exciting?"

"You betcha!"

Greg swirled his spoon through the bowl, his gaze on the melting ice cream. "Funny you should talk about buying a house. I've bought one myself."

"Really?" Renee handed Travis a napkin to wipe away the chocolate ringing his mouth. The idea of Greg leaving the apartment complex—no longer being her neighbor—brought back the familiar old feeling of losing a friend. Crazy. She rarely saw him at home but saw him every day at work. Why would she think anything of it? "Where is this house?"

"In Mountain Hollow." Greg chuckled. "I figure the best way to sell the development is to live there."

"It's a beautiful area." Perfect, in fact.

"It is, isn't it? I'll close in a few weeks. Right now, I'm in the process of—" His gaze dropped to his watch, and he laid the spoon in the bowl. "Oh, man. Time has gotten away from me. I'm supposed to meet the builder at the house in ten minutes."

"Well . . ."

She and Travis had ridden to the restaurant with Greg. The school parking lot, where she'd left her car, was in the opposite direction of the subdivision. He didn't have the time to take her back there without keeping the builder waiting. And she didn't relish dragging Travis along on a long walk in the heat.

"I'm sorry and feel like an idiot." Greg pulled his wallet from his back pocket. "Evidently, the carpet I picked is on back order—for months—and he wants to show me what he says is comparable before he goes out of town on Monday. I picked up a few samples myself this morning. If I don't approve something today, it throws the whole schedule off."

"I understand."

"It shouldn't take long. You can go with me or wait here. Either way, I'll get you back to your car as soon as possible." He paused, a sudden look of desperation darkening his eyes. "I know I'm imposing, and you probably have other things to do, but it would be nice to get a woman's opinion. Maybe you can give me some thoughts about furnishings, too?"

It wasn't that she had anything pressing at home, but the idea of giving him advice on furnishing a house for another woman to occupy in the future made the ice cream curdle in her stomach.

"Can we go, Momma?"

Two pairs of male eyes stared at Renee, waiting for a decision. What could she say?

Renee finished the last of her ice cream and backed her chair from the table. "I'm ready to go if you are."

* * *

On the short drive to Mountain Hollow, Greg said, "I made a deal with the Claytons."

Renee turned on the plush leather seat of his Cadillac, her eyes wide at the news. "When?"

"They called, and I went to see them Thursday afternoon. They've closed the greenhouse and are ready to move to Georgia to live near their daughter. They know it's in their best interest, but it was a hard decision for them."

"I'm sure it was." She lamented the loss of their land and business, but the hard-working, elderly couple deserved to live the remainder of their years in comfort.

Greg drummed his fingers on the padded steering wheel. "On Monday, I'd like you to set up a meeting to start preliminary plans for the land. Try to make it Tuesday afternoon, and include

Adam in the discussion."

"I'll call his secretary first thing." Adam Kessler was their consulting engineer. He'd worked closely with Greg to plan Mountain Hollow.

"Good. I want to create a place that will let the Claytons rest easy, knowing we've treated their property with care and respect."

Oh, was there anything this man could do or say that would prove he was a flawed human being?

"Thanks."

Golden words on a red brick sign announced the entrance to the Mountain Hollow subdivision. It had been a while since she had driven the gently rolling streets. The number of houses lining both sides had grown, and a few people had already moved in. It shouldn't surprise her. After all, the company had sold almost two-thirds of the fifty-two lots, and builders didn't buy them to leave them sitting vacant.

Homes surrounded by trees stood in various stages of completion. Greg's contract stated each lot would remain at least twenty-five percent wooded where possible. He had done a top-notch job with the development and she had no doubt he would do the same on the property owned by the Claytons.

Most of the homes they passed were around two thousand to twenty-five hundred square feet—a veritable mansion compared to Renee's apartment. Ranch homes. Contemporary structures. Brick. Wood siding. One story. Two story. While deed restrictions existed and Dave saw to it that builders followed them to the letter, the variety of styles meant Mountain Hollow could never be called a cookie-cutter development.

Greg parked in a driveway alongside a white pickup truck. In a moment, he was out of his car and opening her door. "Here it is."

Renee climbed from the Seville and eyed the farmhouse-style home with its wrap-around porch and three dormers that indicated rooms on a second floor. Painted a greenish gray, in a few years the place would melt into the trees surrounding it.

Renee opened the door for Travis and unbuckled him while her boss went to the back of the car.

Travis stood on the driveway, his jaw hanging. "Is this Mr. Greg's new house?"

Greg joined them, holding carpet samples he'd retrieved from the trunk. "What do you think, Travis?"

"It's big."

And just Renee's style. She'd always loved the country look. Her mind had first conjured the word *homey*, followed by *comfortable* and *inviting*. Even though houses flanked it on either side, this was a place to relax and enjoy the peace of mountain living. A momentary streak of envy flashed through her, but she refused to let it take hold. "It's incredible."

She stopped on the sidewalk and surveyed what she could see of the wrap-around porch. "I'm already imagining small tables and rocking chairs set strategically for conversation. Possibly a hammock on the side porch? You could hold a party out here."

"I do like the idea of a hammock for relaxing."

"Do you mind if I'm honest?"

"I'd prefer it." Still, his expression turned wary.

"I'm having a hard time picturing you as someone who likes this style of architecture."

He laughed. "You saw me in a contemporary with sharp angles and lots of glass?"

She studied him. "No. More like a traditional brick and stone ranch on a golf course."

"A mix of sentimental and snooty?"

"I wouldn't call it snooty. Sophisticated."

"I like that better. But golf is not my game."

Renee grinned. "Bowling is."

Greg laughed. "Right."

Travis ran ahead of them and climbed the concrete and stone steps. He skipped across boards stained to match the house and stopped at the end of the porch nearest the driveway, bending to peek through the railing.

Greg looked around. "Actually, this place reminds me of the farmhouse my grandparents owned west of Asheville. They had a large porch like this. We spent many nights there talking, singing, or just looking up at the moon and stars. It's where my grandma sipped sweet tea and snapped beans. Of course, their house was simpler than this one, but I always enjoyed spending summers there."

"I'm glad you have those memories." She wished she had some of the same. "This place is beautiful."

Smiling as though she'd given him a gift, he approached the front door. "I kept my eye on this lot. See the slope and trees? It's perfect for a house with a full basement such as this one."

Renee cast a glance at Travis, decided her son was fine, and mounted the steps. "You would never know it had a basement by looking at it from the front."

The door opened to reveal a middle-aged man wearing oversized square glasses that made his thin face even thinner. He thrust out a hand for Greg to shake. "Good to see you, Greg."

"Good to see you, too, Joe. I'm sorry I'm late. I lost track of time this afternoon."

The builder turned to Renee, confusion in his eyes. "Joe Cummings. Mrs. Holmes? Bet you're eager to move in."

"Oh, but—" Mr. Cummings was one of the few builders Renee had never met. Greg raised his brows, like he waited to see how she'd handle the situation. "It's nice to meet you, Mr. Cummings. I'm Mrs. Burnette. I work for Mr. Holmes. Please call me Renee."

"Will do, Renee." The man grinned, obviously unfazed by learning of his error. "I wondered why Greg hadn't invited me to the wedding."

Her boss laughed, and she breathed easier. "Renee is a finalist in the An Apple a Day Bake-off. After today's event, she agreed to help me decide on the carpeting." He held up the samples. "I picked a few more possibilities."

Mr. Cummings motioned for Renee and Travis to step into the foyer. They moved to one side to let Greg and the builder pass.

Hardwood floors led into a dining room to the right and a living area ahead. To the left an L-shaped staircase rose to a second floor, the treads bare and waiting for carpet. Fresh paint scented the air from walls covered in a warm cream color. It almost overwhelmed the smell of wood stain from the trim and doors.

Everyone followed Greg as he strode the short hall into the living area, their footfalls echoing on the bare plywood flooring. He dropped each sample with a *thump* on the wood. Mr. Cummings dropped another sample alongside Greg's.

"What do you think, Renee?" Hands planted on his hips, Greg peered at her as though the splendor of the home's interior rested on her opinion.

She scanned the room's colors—the same as the foyer—and caught her breath as her gaze settled on the fireplace along the back wall of the room. Its stone façade ran all the way up to the ceiling. Light taupe, cream, variants of gray. Other stones leaned toward a faint mossy color that reminded her of the exterior of the house. The fireplace was the focal point of the room now, and she suspected it would remain the focal point once Greg filled the room with furniture.

She stooped to study the samples. They were similar in style, all a short shag. In the first one, though, a thin vein of hunter green wove through a sage color to form a geometric pattern. Two of them, including Mr. Cummings's, leaned toward a chocolate brown with no pattern. The last was a beige color with a green undertone.

Travis crouched beside her. "I like these." He pointed to the brown samples.

Greg stood next to Renee's son and leaned over, hands on his knees. "Why those, Travis?"

"Because they look like huge candy bars," he said, spurring a chuckle from the adults.

Which one would she prefer if this were her house?

Decision made, Renee pushed to her feet, bringing Travis and the beige sample up with her. "I know green is popular, but I think the pattern in the sage is too distracting. The chocolate might work but it will darken the room. If it were up to me, I'd choose this one." She held out the beige sample. "The neutral shade reflects some of the color in the stone but fades into the background and will allow the spotlight to shine on that beautiful wall with the windows and fireplace."

Renee waited a few moments, her heart hammering while Mr. Cummings looked to Greg for his opinion. Her boss folded his arms and glanced from the sample to the fireplace and back to the sample.

She couldn't stand it any longer. "Of course, as a man, you think it's too bland or feminine."

"No. Actually, you made some great points." He turned to Joe Cummings. "I like it. Let's go with it."

The builder took the sample from Renee. "I'll get it ordered and installed."

"Appreciate it." Greg smiled at her. "And thanks, Renee. How about a tour of the rest of the house?"

"I'd love it."

Mr. Cummings held out the key to the door. "I have to meet my guys on lot six. Just drop this by on your way out, if you would."

"Sure." Greg took the key. After the builder left, he swept out a hand. "Now that we've resolved the carpet issue, what furnishing ideas do you have for this space?"

"If money were no object?" she teased.

He laughed. "Well, try to keep it within reason."

Renee stood about a third of the way into the large room and studied it. Soon, her imagination ran wild. "I think a leather couch here, a plush chair and table in that corner." She pointed across the room to a space under the window, left of the fireplace. "For reading."

She moved forward and to the right of the make-believe couch and did a half-turn. "I can see a recliner here for watching television." She pointed to the wall opposite where she stood. "I think a nice oak entertainment center there."

"I can see myself with my feet propped up, watching a Falcons game."

She could see him, too.

Renee cleared her throat and faced the back of the room again. "The stone fireplace and the windows on either side provide a rustic appearance." Another pair of windows above followed the vaulted ceiling on either side of the stone, providing good light to the room. "I'd add some decorative pieces that reflect a country farmhouse style. Maybe an old pitcher with dried flowers, some candlesticks or an oil lamp for the mantel. You might consider a basket or a set of crock jars in various sizes to sit on the hearth.

"Oh, you have to hang a landscape painting or print on that stone. Maybe something with a mountain scene or . . ." She turned back to him. "Do you know the art of Bob Timberlake?"

"Not that I'm aware."

"He's very good and a North Carolina artist. I can definitely see . . ." Renee caught the sparkle in Greg's eyes and the pucker of his lips as he restrained a laugh. "I've gotten carried away, haven't I?"

"Maybe a little." He laughed. "Don't worry. My invitation for your thoughts was sincere. Home decorating isn't my strong suit."

He didn't cook. He didn't decorate. He wasn't perfect after all. But he was so close.

They entered the master bedroom with French doors that opened onto a sitting room, then another pair of French doors that led to a sunroom overlooking the backyard. "I think my whole apartment would fit into these rooms."

He showed her the upstairs, where Travis embarrassed her by picking out a bedroom for himself. They peeked into every nook and cranny, then took the stairs to the basement with its long bar for entertaining and . . . another stone fireplace.

After they had seen every inch and Renee had provided him with her decorating tips, Greg practically ran back up the stairs. Excitement exuded from him. "I've saved the best for last."

They entered the large breakfast room attached to an even larger kitchen with honey oak cabinets and all the counter space she could ever hope to employ, and more French doors that opened onto a side porch. And double ovens!

"I'm going to say by that look of wonder on your face that it meets your approval?" Enjoyment permeated Greg's voice.

Her lips parted to say it was more than she'd ever dreamed

of having. That this house made the house she had wanted in Orchard Valley look like a shack. Fortunately, no words escaped. How could she say all that knowing a place like this—his place—would never be hers?

"Is there a swing set in the backyard, Mr. Greg?"

"Not yet, Travis. Maybe one day."

"And a dog."

Greg ruffed her son's hair. "And a dog."

One day a swing set. One day a dog. Kids. A wife.

This house was too large for a single man. He must have someone in mind to occupy it with him. Picturing Greg coming home each day to a family wrenched Renee's heart in a way she hadn't expected. She'd known her feelings for him were growing stronger by the day, however, she hadn't anticipated this rush of—

No. What good would it do to name it? He had admitted he didn't need the trouble that could arise from an office romance, and neither did she.

Renee reached for Travis's hand. "We've enjoyed the tour, but we should head home."

The light of pleasure in Greg's eyes dimmed. "Oh. Sure. I should return the key to Joe, anyway."

She hurried down the porch steps, opened the car door for Travis and buckled him in, then straightened and turned to Greg, who held the front passenger door open for her. "This house really is lovely." She took one last lingering gaze at the place, wondering if desire shown in her eyes. "I think you'll be very happy here."

"Renee . . ."

"Yes?" As his stare held hers, time and all motion seemed to stop. Her heartbeat pounded in her ears. She hadn't experienced a bond like this in years.

Then he glanced at Travis in the back seat, breaking their connection. "I'm glad you like it. Thanks for the decorating tips."

Was that really what he'd planned to say? By the seriousness in his tone when he said her name, she didn't think so. But his glance at Travis must have convinced him to not say whatever was on his mind.

Renee climbed in the car. Greg would never know how often during the past hour she had imagined herself living here one day with Travis . . . and Greg.

CHAPTER THIRTEEN

Geneva glided up the side aisle of the sanctuary, a woman comfortable in her identity and relationships with others. A woman who was Renee's opposite. Hadn't she proven that yesterday after snapping at Val? Then she'd nearly run from Greg after he drove her back to her car parked at the high school.

Folding her arms around Renee in a warm hug, Geneva said, "I would have attended the bake-off yesterday, but my son and his family visited from Charlotte. I heard you and Val will move on to the next round. Congratulations."

"Thank you. It was quite a surprise." One that kept her up much of the night as her thoughts spun like a merry-go-round leading to an overwhelming sense of inadequacy. And her conscience still smarted this morning.

During snatches of sleep, dreams flooded her mind, crazy scenes involving Greg, his house, dogs, ice cream, typing, and bowling. Bowling?

People entered the sanctuary in preparation for the Sunday morning service while the organist played "Great is Thy Faithfulness." She spotted Val at the front of the room but on the other side. Renee waved, though it was more an "I have seats over here" kind of gesture than a hello.

Val waved back, a limp motion expressing good manners rather than the usual pleasure in seeing Renee. She poked Pete in the side and pointed to the empty pew a row down, then sat with her family a whole sanctuary away. Normally, one of them would find a pew with enough space for the Sargeants and the Burnettes, something Renee had done this morning—in vain, it appeared.

"I don't want anything to change between us. But what if I have no say in the matter?"

"You always have a say."

Unaware she had mumbled her concern out loud, Geneva's statement startled Renee. "I don't know, Geneva. I said something I shouldn't have yesterday. I would love to be more like you, patient and understanding."

"Honey, you only see me here at church or in social settings like the Culinary Capers meetings. At those times, I'm on my best behavior. But don't mistake that for perfection. I have a temper, you know."

Renee's eyes widened at the confession, trying to imagine Geneva losing her temper with anyone.

"Oh, I'm not abusive, but there are times I let my mouth run over my good sense." Geneva shook her head. "Long ago, I said some horrible things to my sister. What happened to provoke me was my fault, but I lashed out at her anyway."

"We went years before we spoke again, only reconciling as she lay dying from cancer. By then, I had missed out on so much of her life and the lives of her children. It's something I'll always regret. Don't be like me and allow the silence to grow, especially when you're at fault."

Renee bit her bottom lip. "What if I talk until I'm blue in the face but Val won't forgive me?"

"That day at my sister's bedside, I was all blubber and no coherency. Finally, God led me to say the right thing. I'm learning to rely on Him when I get angry." She laughed. "But I'm a work in progress and will be until I take my last breath."

Rely on God. That pinched harder than her Aunt Margaret's effusive greetings. She hugged Geneva. "Thank you for the advice . . . and for not being perfect."

Geneva waved a hand. "My whole family will tell you I'm far from it. It took years, but I've learned that recognizing and accepting my faults is not an excuse to stop trying to be better."

How many times had Renee wished to be like Geneva with her perceived sweet temperament and strong, mature faith? Only, it turned out the woman was as human as Renee. She looked around the sanctuary and realized there wasn't a soul in sight who wasn't a work in progress.

Renee turned to her son. He sat on the pew, kicking his legs back and forth while looking through a picture book. "Come on, Travis. Let's go sit with the Sargeants."

As the organist played the last bars of the prelude, Renee and Travis wriggled down the aisle between congregants like salmon swimming upstream. Once they reached Val and her family, Melissa looked up and grinned, one front tooth missing.

The girl elbowed her brother and they both scooted over, allowing room for the Burnettes. The movement caught Val's attention. Renee mouthed "I'm sorry." With a restrained smile and bob of her head, Val shuffled closer to her husband to accommodate the two extra people. Renee almost danced with delight. After the service, she would apologize properly.

Maybe there was hope yet that one day a mature faith would naturally flow from her. For today, she had chosen to not let the silence grow.

Her chest tightened. But what about the next time they discussed the bake-off?

* * *

"Hold up, Renee."

She turned away from her car to see Greg approaching her in the parking lot behind the office building. Freshly-shaved, dark suit, the smell of cologne floating in the morning air. Had a Monday morning ever looked so good on someone?

She wished she could say the same about herself. After Saturday's ice cream outing, then the tour of every square foot of his new house, she'd spent Sunday afternoon pondering the reason for both. Why had he really taken them for ice cream? He hadn't needed to do it. And why ask her opinion of the décor in his house? Her furnishings would hardly recommend her taste.

It all confused her, and she was tired of looking for fanciful motives that weren't there. It simply boiled down to the fact that he was a good boss—a good man—who hoped to relate to his employees rather than consider himself above them. Wasn't that why he'd formed the bowling team?

Renee put on her best smile. "Good morning."

"Good morning." Greg walked alongside her to the rear door of the office and laid a hand on her arm, stopping her before she could go inside. "I'd like to talk to you. Why don't you get settled, then come to my office. Say, twenty minutes?" He opened the door and stood back, letting her step inside first.

His voice had taken on a serious note. Rather than worry over the idea that she'd done something wrong, Renee placated herself with the thought that he had tasks for her to do. This was probably how it would be until he'd found a replacement for Nora.

Or . . .

With Nora officially gone, this might be the time he offered Renee the job. For weeks, she had imagined him calling her into his office. He would say something like, "Renee, I believe you'll make a great replacement for Nora. How would you like the job?"

She should have taken the initiative long ago to approach him, but now her heart rate kicked up at the possibility. "Yes, sir."

Once she reached her desk, she slipped her purse in a drawer and checked for notes from Dave or Jim. Finding nothing, she walked to the kitchen and poured a cup of coffee from the pot Colleen had made. A slight tremor ran through her hand, causing the pot to wobble. Fortunately, it wasn't full and didn't slosh hot coffee to burn her skin.

She took the coffee to her little corner of the building, calling out a "Good morning" as she passed the offices of her coworkers. Once settled in the chair, she checked her slim Timex watch. Eight minutes to go. The tips of her fingernails drummed the wood surface of the desk. That didn't leave time to do much more than drink coffee and turn on the typewriter. And it was too early to call Adam Kessler to set up an appointment for tomorrow.

Jim popped out of his office, a stack of papers in his hands, which he passed to her. "Will you make me three copies, please?"

"Do you need them right away?" She checked her watch again. "I'm supposed to report to Greg in a couple of minutes."

"In that case, it can wait." His eyebrows dipped. "You'll probably be pretty busy until Greg finds a new secretary."

Renee couldn't stop the wince but told herself it was due to the reminder of an increased workload instead of his belief that she would continue to work for him and Dave. Nora might be gone, but Greg's work hadn't stopped. Since she was the only official secretary left in the office, it was natural she would be called on to take up the slack, and she intended to do it to the best of her ability, promotion or not.

She laid the papers down, grabbed her steno pad, and stood.

"I'll manage. And I'll make those copies as soon as I get back to my desk."

"Thanks. Dave and I know we can count on you."

One indrawn breath later, she walked along the hall for the fourth time in twenty minutes and stepped into Nora's old office. Even with the furniture still in place, it looked empty and abandoned without papers on the desk and the lush, welcoming plants.

She knocked on Greg's door and opened it after hearing, "Come in."

He had removed the suit jacket, hung it on a chrome coat rack in the corner, and now sat behind his desk, his own cup of steaming coffee in front of him. Looking up, he said, "You can shut the door and have a seat, Renee."

She took her place in the chair in front of the desk and situated herself to take dictation or note any tasks he wished to give her.

"You won't need that." He pointed to the pen and steno pad.

"Oh. All right."

She did her best to relax but figured her nervousness showed. Nervousness. Excitement. Anticipation. Dread. All the emotions swirled inside her like leaves in a whirlwind.

Leaning back in his chair, hands folded over his middle, Greg's blue-gray gaze pierced her, holding her captive. "I wanted to reiterate that I thought you did an excellent job planning Nora's party."

"I was happy to help." Oh, she felt as though she were riding a roller coaster of expectancy, eager to see if this morning would be the time he would mention a promotion for her. Right now, she was chugging toward the apex.

"I realize you work hard now, Renee, but I'll need you to

work harder until a new secretary can be found."

Until a new secretary can be found.

Just like that, her stomach fell as the roller coaster crested the top and plunged. He hadn't said a new secretary for him, though, had he?

She held her breath, waiting for him to continue. *Just spit everything out!*

He was killing her.

Greg's telephone buzzed. He frowned and asked her to answer.

She reached out to pick up the receiver and punched the lit button. "Greg Holmes's office."

"Nora?"

She recognized the voice. "No, Pam, this is Renee Burnette."

"Hi, Renee. I'm sorry. I forgot Nora retired. Have you taken her place?"

Renee glanced at Greg. "Um . . . no."

"Well, Adam is calling for Mr. Holmes."

"Just a moment, please." She pressed the "Hold" button. "Adam Kessler would like to talk to you. I haven't had a chance to set up that appointment with him."

Greg straightened and reached for the receiver. "I'll take care of it and save you a phone call."

While he spoke with their outside engineer about the new development, Renee mulled over his words to her. He expected her to work harder until he hired a new secretary. For Dave and Jim? She liked working for the men, but it was her responsibility to look out for herself and her son.

"Let's meet," Greg checked his calendar, "tomorrow at 2:00? . . . Okay. See you then." He hung up the phone and wrote the meeting on his desk calendar. "You probably figured out from my end of the conversation that we'll meet here tomorrow, then I'll take Kessler on a tour of the Clayton property."

No, she hadn't. She'd been too focused on what he'd said before the call to hear anything more than the time. *Pay attention, Renee.* "I'll make a note on my calendar and let Jim and Dave know."

"Good." Greg leaned forward and folded his arms on the desk. "I can't operate for long without an assistant—"

Her stomach tumbled, and she fought a smile. This was it.

"—but until I find that person, I want you to know how much I appreciate what you do around here and how much I value you as a temporary secretary to me."

The roller coaster she'd ridden for weeks stopped cold, nearly throwing her out of the metaphoric car. Temporary? He didn't plan to ask her, which meant . . .

She had to know. "Are you aware that Colleen is interested in the position?"

He sighed. "She approached me about it on Friday. I told her I didn't think she was ready. I need someone with more experience."

It was no consolation that Greg had bypassed Colleen. And it didn't mean Renee's effort was over. She had experience. Hadn't he said a few minutes ago that he could count on her? What stopped him from doing so, permanently?

His lips curled up in a smile. "Let's get back to you. Nora suggested a raise, and I agreed. In the seven months you've been here, you've shown your ability to handle the jobs you've been given. I think it's time you were compensated accordingly."

"Thank you." She could express her gratitude, so why didn't she feel it?

Once he named a figure, Renee did some quick math in her head, and her shoulders fell, along with her expectations. It would help when it came to house payments but wasn't as much as she would have anticipated receiving were she to fill Nora's shoes.

She swallowed. "That's generous."

Her back straightened. How likely was it that she would get the position she sought by sitting numb and silent? For years, she had gone along to get along. She was tired of being the one expected to give in to everyone else's wishes and demands. She was tired of not standing on her own two feet and making *her* wishes known. It was time to stop acting as though her future depended solely upon him. It was time to come right out and demand . . . no, *ask*—strongly and with confidence—that he consider her as his new assistant.

"Greg, I wanted to talk to you—"

The phone buzzed again. Renee's hands itched to pick it up and toss it out the window behind her boss.

"I'll get it this time." Greg answered the phone. "Greg Holmes . . . Thanks, Colleen. I'll send Renee for her." He hung up. "My appointment is here. Her name is Helen Peters. Will you bring her back?"

"Of course." She opened her mouth to say, "In a minute," but shut it again.

"Thanks." He pulled a folder from a stack on his desk and gave the contents his full attention.

She rose from her seat. Dismissed. He hadn't even asked what she wanted to talk to him about. Had he even heard her?

She sighed. At least she'd gotten a raise out of the meeting.

As Renee walked down the hall toward the reception area to retrieve Ms. Peters, her steps faltered. The time she and Greg spent together on Saturday—the ice cream, the house tour . . . Was her raise meant to assist her in finding her own house? The thought left her teetering between a desire to kiss him for his thoughtfulness and wring his neck over disappointing her in her wish to earn it.

After escorting Greg's visitor to his office, Renee returned to her desk.

Colleen appeared in the doorway between Renee's hole-in-the-hall and the reception area. "You look frustrated."

She painted on a smile. "I'm fine."

"I wonder if she'll be the one."

"The one?"

"To take Nora's place."

Renee's gaze shot down the hall. "You mean she's the—"

"The next interviewee."

She should have guessed. The smug grin creasing Colleen's face stomped on Renee's last nerve. In the background, she heard the phone ringing. "Isn't it your job to answer the phones?"

Colleen scowled, then whipped around and disappeared.

Renee snatched up Jim's paperwork and marched down the hall on her way to the file room where the copy machine was housed. She slowed near her boss's office, hoping to hear a portion of the conversation with Ms. Peters. The voices were too low, though laughter met her ears.

As she raised and lowered the lid on the copier, hearing the whir of the machine, her mind kept returning to the woman she'd escorted to Greg's office. Would Helen Peters become their newest employee?

CHAPTER FOURTEEN

The front door opened and Marie invited Renee inside her small ranch-style house. "Come in."

Renee followed her into the den with its red-brick fireplace that dominated one wall. Reddish-brown paneling covered the rest of the room. Evening sunlight beamed through a large window in the breakfast area to the right, casting a yellow glow over the table and chairs.

After saying hello to Geneva and Shelley, who sat side-by-side on a seventies sofa upholstered in shades of orange and brown, Renee chose a spot on a matching loveseat. Both furniture pieces formed an L-shape with a small table dividing them in the corner.

Marie walked toward the kitchen off the breakfast area, a galley kitchen like Renee's, but wider and twice as long. She returned a moment later and handed Renee a glass of tea, then left to answer the doorbell.

Laughter and multiple voices announced Val and Darlene's arrival. Val settled on the other end of the loveseat. Renee smiled at her, thankful she had apologized for her caustic comment at the bake-off. It seemed *caustic* was her middle name lately, even at work. First, she jumped down Colleen's throat, then she'd snapped at Debbie for committing a benign but irritating accounting mistake. If she wasn't careful, Greg would take back his raise. Worse, she would lose precious friends.

Meeting with Greg on Monday had added the equivalent of lighter fluid to Renee's dream, causing an inferno of renewed desire for a house. It hadn't helped that his busy week had prevented her from pinning him down for another conversation. It looked as though winning the bake-off was her only option in obtaining her dream.

"Aren't we proud of Renee and Val for making it to the final round of the bake-off?" Geneva grinned. "You two must be excited."

Shelley set her glass of tea on a coaster on the corner table. "Are you nervous? I can't imagine the pressure of having to bake a dish in front of a group of people who will judge every little thing—taking off for this and taking off for that."

"Well, I wasn't nervous before you mentioned it." Val grinned. "I'm sure it won't be any different than baking in front of y'all."

Renee couldn't agree with her but didn't say so. Thinking about that final round, the one that would determine how soon she could meet her goal, introduced a swarm of ballerinas so active in her stomach she imagined their pirouettes. What if she became nervous and added the wrong ingredient or the wrong amount? What if she got distracted and let what she baked overcook or burn? What if she—

"What about you, Renee? Are you nervous?"

Her lips turned up into what she hoped was a confident smile. "Actually, this week has been busy at work, and I haven't had much time to focus on the bake-off."

Val turned sideways and gazed at her. "So, you still don't know what you'll prepare?"

"Not yet. Outside of work, I've put aside efforts to test recipes in favor of spending time with Travis."

Truthfully, her child had become more and more rebellious

and mouthy, constantly berating apples and the bake-off, along with complaining about everything from the clothes she laid out for him to the temperature of his bathwater. "I'll have more time to think about my entry over the weekend."

"Has Greg offered you Nora's position yet?" Val sipped her iced tea.

Renee's grip on her own cold glass tightened. "No. He hasn't."

"I wonder why?"

Heat ran through Renee from her head to the tips of her toes. The room went quiet with the rest of the women looking everywhere but at the two of them. Based on the insincerity of the question in Val's voice, they probably thought Renee hadn't been promoted because her work wasn't up to snuff.

The cushions on the loveseat rolled when Val shifted her position, uncrossing then recrossing her legs, as though she, too, struggled with her comment.

Bear with each other and forgive one another if any of you has a grievance against someone. Forgive as the Lord forgave you.

Renee had memorized the verse in Colossians as part of her Sunday school lesson. Now, it roared at her. But, in this case, what did a lack of forgiveness look like? She had a feeling it looked too much like the polite smiles she and Val were exchanging right now.

How could she ever hope to become strong but humble in her faith if she relied on her own wavering emotions and not the Holy Spirit? Val was still her friend, and though things were strained lately, she would do what she could to make sure that friendship never ended.

The sooner they got past the An Apple A Day Bake-off, the better.

* * *

Renee arrived at work on Friday still thinking of her embarrassment at the meeting last night. While Val had been cordial throughout the cooking portion of their time together and right up to the moment they said goodbye to one another, none of the usual spontaneous teasing or boisterous laughter burst from either of them. It was as though a cloud of gloom hung over their heads.

Grabbing her purse from under her desk, Renee opened her wallet and checked to see how much cash she had. Eighteen dollars. Although she should save it for any last-minute school supplies for Travis or purchasing whatever ingredients she would need to experiment with new recipes, she had another purpose in mind for part of the money.

She picked up the phone, dialed the bank down the street, and asked for Val. When she heard her friend answer, she swallowed her nerves. "Val, it's Renee."

"Hi."

Despite the coolness between them, Renee forced some pep in her voice. "I called to see if you'd like to go to lunch with me today."

A long pause. "I really can't. Pete has me on a strict budget."

Since when had Val paid any attention to her husband's financial requests? Not since Renee had known her.

If she was sincere in her desire to be a forgiving friend . . . "I'll buy."

"That isn't necessary." A drawn-out sigh came over the line. "Sure. Gully's?"

The rock in Renee's chest dissolved. "Sounds good. I'll meet you there at noon."

"Okay."

She hung up and checked her watch. Hopefully, by one o'clock, they would be back in one another's good graces.

At 12:09 Renee rushed into the restaurant, stopping near the door to look for Val. She found her seated in a booth off to the side, menu open on the table in front of her. Renee slipped onto the vinyl-covered bench across from her friend and opened her own menu. "I'm sorry I'm late. Greg called me into his office at the last minute to dictate a couple of letters."

"It's okay. I've been deciding what I'll have."

The woman who waited on Greg, Renee, and Travis last Saturday stepped up to the table, set down two water glasses, and pulled her order pad from her little black apron. She smiled at seeing Renee. "Well, hey there. I don't see you in here much, then you're in twice in a week's time."

"It's nice to see you again. Jeanie, right?"

"Right. You know, I didn't catch your name when you came in over the weekend. I like to know the names of our regulars."

"Renee Burnette." She pointed to Val, hoping to distract the waitress from mentioning that she'd come to the restaurant with Greg. "This is Val Sargeant."

Jeanie turned her smile on Val. "Nice to meet you. What can I get y'all?"

After they each ordered a salad and half-sandwich, Jeanie scooped up the menus and left. The women chatted about minor things until the waitress returned and set their meals in front of them. "Can I get you anything else?"

Val shook her head, and Renee said, "No, thanks."

"Enjoy, ladies, and you tell Mr. Holmes he's welcome to bring you and that cute little boy in here anytime."

As Jeanie walked away, the burn built on Renee's face, amplified by Val's slack jaw.

"What did she mean by that?"

Renee shrugged and busied herself mixing bleu cheese dressing through her salad, hoping to leave Val's question unanswered.

Her friend stared her down. "That shrug wasn't an answer to my question."

"Greg brought us here for ice cream last Saturday. It was nothing." On the contrary, last Saturday's house tour was something she had thought about off and on all week. She had especially rerun the memory of that stare between them, one that spoke of promise and infinitely more than an employer/employee relationship.

"After the competition?"

"Yes."

"Why didn't you tell me? We're best friends."

"It was no big deal, Val. Just a celebra—" No, that probably wasn't a good topic to bring up. "We had ice cream, talked for a few minutes, and left."

"I can't believe you came here with Greg Holmes and didn't say something." Val gasped. "Unless that was why you asked me to lunch. Oh, that blush on your face says last Saturday involved more than ice cream. What happened after you left? Did he ask you out? Are you planning to go out with him . . . without Travis?"

Renee waved off Val's questions as if her friend made much over nothing. She stabbed at the lettuce on her plate, then a cherry tomato. "He's buying a house and needed to meet the builder to approve a carpet choice. When he realized he was running late and didn't have time to drop us back at the school, he asked that we come along. He wanted my thoughts about the carpet."

Val bit into her sandwich and chewed thoughtfully. Finally, she swallowed. "Wow. What was it like?"

"What?"

"The house, silly."

Renee set her fork on the plate and crossed her arms on the table, ready to tell her friend all about the place. "Oh, Val, it was beautiful. It's in our Mountain Hollow subdivision." She spent the next five minutes describing the place from the basement to the bedrooms. "Everything about it is perfect."

Having finished her sandwich, Val dug into her salad. "Let me remind you that, unless the woman is his mother, when a man asks for a woman's *thoughts* on something like that, he isn't taking a random survey. He wants to know if she'd be happy living there."

Val's words flew like Cupid's arrow to pierce Renee's heart as she recalled Greg's eagerness to hear her suggestions for the house, his laughter over Travis choosing a bedroom, and the comment about the dog in the backyard.

"Who wouldn't?" Renee sucked in a breath. She said that out loud? "But that's ridiculous. He's my boss, not my . . . boyfriend." Could it be that Saturday was Greg's way of testing her interest in him?

"You know what I mean. Be more assertive. The Women's Liberation Movement wasn't started by bashful females."

"I'm not a feminist, Val. But I guess I can agree that I'm modern enough in my thinking to believe I would be free to approach him *if* I thought he meant anything personal by seeking out my opinion. I'm also old-fashioned enough to want a man to ask me out first, something Greg has not done."

"All I'm suggesting is that you give him a chance."

Their conversation progressed to kids and school and the new shopping center being built a quarter mile outside of downtown. They laughed and complained and shared a little benign gossip.

Renee hadn't approached Val with the reason for the lunch—to be sure their friendship wouldn't suffer permanent damage from the stress of the bake-off. They'd shared such a pleasurable, normal time together that she decided she wouldn't spoil the fellowship by bringing up what had become a divisive subject.

But for the rest of the day, Val's suggestion to give Greg a romantic chance wouldn't leave Renee alone. What had he really intended to say as she prepared to leave his new house on Saturday? Whatever it was, he hadn't brought up the visit again.

That arrow twisted, digging deep in her chest.

CHAPTER FIFTEEN

Even in the open air near the apartment's playground, apples remained the dominant scent for Renee. How could she escape a smell that had saturated her pores. Apples and cinnamon. Apples and sugar. Apples and dough. Baked apples. Fried apples. The list went on. She'd spent all weekend baking and listening to her son's complaints. Finally, yesterday after church, she took Travis to his grandparents to save them both hours of torture.

This evening, she sat on the bench while Travis played, her eyes on her son, but her thoughts focused on the bake-off. With the memory of an enjoyable lunch with Val still fresh in her mind, she'd come to dread the final round. Was a threat to their friendship worth the effort? She could remain in her apartment until she'd saved—

"Hi, Renee."

She jumped at Greg's voice. Turning toward the sound, she spotted him at the edge of the playground, waiting as though seeking her permission to cross the grass. "Hi."

That was all it took. He strolled toward her, grinning. "I saw you from my apartment."

Renee squelched the immediate instinct to glance toward the building where he lived.

He pointed to the bench. "Mind if I join you?"

She scooted a little closer to the edge, and he sat down, keeping a space between them. "You looked like you were into some heavy thinking before I interrupted."

Futile thinking. "I'm still searching for a recipe for the final round of the competition."

"How's it coming?"

"Not well, frankly."

"You'll figure it out."

"Hi, Mr. Greg!" Travis waved to him from the swing set.

"Hi, Travis!" Greg turned his attention from the swings back to Renee. "He's having fun."

"He loves coming to the playground." Renee leaned closer. "Don't say anything, but I think he has a crush on the little girl on the other swing."

"Six and already a lady's man." Greg's deep chuckle had her smiling. "Any problems at the office today?"

Was that why he'd come out here? To talk about work? "Everything went fine, no fires to put out."

"Good. You're getting along okay . . . with the workload, I mean? I'm not keeping you too busy, am I?"

"Busy, yes, but nothing I can't handle." Renee angled toward him and crossed her legs as she pondered taking advantage of the moment. *Be assertive.* She fisted her hands together in her lap and prayed for courage. "I had hoped to talk to you about something."

The back of the wooden bench squeaked as he leaned against it. "Go ahead."

"I don't want to sound nosey, but I've wondered if you hired Ms. Peters."

"No. She's an excellent candidate, though."

"You're still considering her?"

"I'll interview a few others before making up my mind."

"Then Nora's position is still open?"

"Why are you asking?" His expression turned guarded,

slightly weakening her courage. "I thought you said you were doing fine with the workload."

Her backbone stiffened with the determination to assert herself and speak the truth. "It has nothing to do with too much work. You've interviewed candidates from outside the office."

Had that last part sounded as resentful to him as it had to her? He'd already admitted Ms. Peters was an excellent candidate for a job Renee believed should be hers. Then there had been Miss August. Thankfully, the drop-dead gorgeous pin-up girl would not work with Greg—*day after day*. His integrity allowed him to see the danger she would present.

"I would like to be considered for the position."

His eyes widened and he sat straight. "Renee—"

"It isn't that I'm unappreciative of the raise you gave me, but I believe I'm as capable of doing the job as anyone else—"

"So do I."

"—I've tried to prove it to you these past weeks." Renee blinked several times as his words registered. "You do?"

"I do. If not, I would never have handed you the job of organizing Nora's party rather than giving it to Colleen or Debbie."

Then why not choose her as his new secretary? She tried to lighten the conversation. "Does that also apply to organizing the bowling team?"

Greg dipped his head, no longer looking her in the eye. "Yes and no."

What did that mean?

Rather than try to satisfy her curiosity, Renee returned to the original topic. "I assumed that if you considered me qualified, you would have offered me the job."

"My mom drilled into me to never make assumptions." He graced her with a smile, probably an effort to relieve some of the tension between them. It didn't work for Renee. He cleared his throat. "Sorry. I've always thought you were over-qualified for your current position, and to be honest, Nora suggested you as a good choice to fill her shoes."

Nora made that suggestion? Renee shook her head, confused. "Then will you at least tell me why you disagreed?"

"I didn't disagree." Greg sprang to his feet, causing the old bench to bounce and Renee to flinch at the sudden movement. He shoved his hands in the pockets of his jeans, took a couple of steps forward, then spun to face her. Whatever he wanted to say, the somber look on his face meant it was important. "If the circumstances were different, I would have asked you before she even left. As things are for me, I was reluctant to place you . . . or maybe it's only me . . . in a difficult position."

"What difficult position?"

"I . . . well, I've tried to get up the courage to ask something else of you." He pushed a hand through his hair, and a nerve at the side of his mouth jumped, stretching his lips into what resembled a nervous twitch. Renee's stomach tumbled in response. "These last couple of months have been harder than I imagined, Renee. I can't work closely with you day after day and pretend I'm only interested in an office relationship between us."

Renee's head spun as she tried to absorb his statement. Her heartbeat nearly choked her with its intensity. "You mean—"

His brow creased, and he raised a hand to stop her. "Please don't get the wrong idea. I've never believed a romantic relationship among employees resulted in anything good, especially when one member of the couple was the boss. If things go south, it creates an uncomfortable situation for both people."

We agree on that point.

"But something happened that I couldn't ignore."

"What?"

"While doing paperwork at home one Saturday in June, I got up to stretch and looked out the window. I saw you here with Travis. He'd hurt himself on the playground and started crying. Blood dripped down his leg. The way you calmed him and got him laughing in no time . . ."

Her gaze shot to his apartment window without hesitation. She remembered that afternoon but hadn't realized he was watching. The cut on Travis's knee had bled like water from a faucet. Thank goodness she hadn't passed out, since the sight of blood tends to make her lightheaded. She'd debated taking him to the doctor but after inspecting the wound, found it wasn't deep or serious. After the initial shock, she'd told him a silly joke, and they both laughed.

Greg shook his head. "I guess most mothers would do the same as you, but I saw how much you loved your son. After that, I paid more attention to you—here and at work." A chuckle escaped. "Not in a creepy way, I promise. But you've weighed on my mind. I've prayed about it, and over time, tried to forget any notion of asking you out. It's done no good, and I feel the same way I've felt for weeks. More so, if you want to know the truth. You asked about the bowling team. I thought if we spent time together away from the office—but not alone—I would discover we weren't compatible."

Renee attempted to move, to say something. Her muscles refused to cooperate while she wrapped her mind around the confirmation of Val's claim that Greg had feelings for her on a personal level. Part of her wished to jump up and shout for joy. She restrained the impulse for the same reason he had shown restraint in asking her out. It was too risky, right?

He stared at the ground, then the swings. "Now you're uncomfortable."

"No, just surprised."

But why? Even without Val's encouragement, she had suspected his interest before now. She had seen it but denied it as being a fanciful impression brought on by her growing interest in him. Yet, was she willing to endanger her job, maybe her future plans, for the possibility that things would work out between them?

"You told me you didn't hire Miss August . . ." She really needed to stop referring to the woman that way. "You told me you didn't hire her because you didn't want the problems associated with an office fling."

"That's true, but she was flirting for a reason other than an interest in me as a person."

"I'm glad to hear you saw through it, because I wouldn't want a man who found those shallow types of relationships appealing."

He smiled down at her. "Are you saying a man like me might interest you . . ." he held his hand up, thumb and forefinger an inch apart, "a little bit?"

Renee's laugh competed with the laughter of children in the background. "Maybe," she duplicated his gesture, "a little bit."

"Then are you willing to explore something more than a working relationship between us?"

The indecision weighed heavily on her, and she could hardly catch her breath. She bit down on her lower lip and studied his face, so handsome and expectant. And she had thought finding a recipe for the bake-off would be the hardest decision she would make this evening.

The longer she pondered the question, the more his smile faded, until the loss of it drove her thoughts from her mouth. "Do you really think we can work together if it—if we—fall apart?"

"The only guarantee I can give you, Renee, is to ask God every day to keep me from doing something stupid."

Prayer could accomplish so much, and after seeing his willingness to pray at Nora's party, she had no doubt he would faithfully do so over their relationship. She only wished she were as faithful in that area. "I'll admit I'm afraid to take the risk when I have to consider Travis. What about my son? Dating someone with a child . . ."

Greg glanced over to where Travis played on the old merry-go-round with Tiffany and her brother. Her son stared at them with curiosity, his head whipping around as the playground piece spun. "He's a great kid."

How could she fight against that?

"Do you mind if I ask what happened to his father?"

"We moved here after Steve left the Army. A few months later, he rode his motorcycle too fast on a winding road and lost control."

"I'm sorry." Greg reached out as if to touch her, then withdrew his hand.

"Me, too." Since Steve's sudden death three years ago, she had struggled to adjust to raising her son alone. Working. Paying the bills. Grieving. "To my shame, I've sometimes railed against God for allowing me to be put in the position of calling myself a widow. Other times, I've railed against Steve for speeding that day. I've also railed against myself over an unreasonable anger with both of them."

His expression softened. "Grief can manifest itself in unreasonable ways, Renee. God knows that."

Her eyes moistened. Could he see the way his uplifting words caused her to glow inside? Almost like the lightning bugs that filled the summer evenings with their flickering radiance.

"Maybe we could start slow? A casual date to see where things take us?"

"Slow and steady?"

"I haven't gone steady since I was in high school." Renee laughed to cover the fact that she'd allowed her nerves to take over her mouth. "Yes. I think that makes sense."

"How about dinner Saturday?"

"I'd like that."

While she could have floated back to her apartment on a cloud of ecstasy, a thought kept her feet grounded. What did this mean for her promotion? A silky, persuasive little voice entered her head.

If things work out between you, you will have no need to buy a house on your own. Greg has seen to it with his purchase of that beauty in Mountain Hollow.

Oh, she did like that house. Was this God's way of making her dream of a permanent home come true?

She frowned. It seemed too much a matter of exploitation of a relationship to her liking. The last thing she wanted was for Greg or anyone else to think she had maneuvered her way into a house or a job. "There is one more thing . . . two, really."

Greg sat beside her on the bench and took her hand, his warm palm lighting a fire of emotion inside her. "Tell me."

"Do we keep this a secret at work? I don't like feeling as if I'm sneaking around and doing something wrong, yet I don't want to cause problems in the office." She could already see Colleen's reaction.

He shook his head. "Each time we talk, I find something new I like about you, Renee. Today, it's your honesty." His brow furrowed. "If things work out as I hope, I think we'll find it hard to keep our dates a secret. It's a small town and we're bound to run into the others at some point. While I don't think it's necessary to send out a memo, I do believe we should keep things professional at the office, no different than it's been. How do you see us handling it?"

She liked that he asked for her opinion. "The same."

"Good." He rubbed his hands together, ready to move on. "What else?"

"There's still the matter of Nora's replacement. Is it settled?"

A light pink hue that had nothing to do with the sun covered both of his cheeks. "I want us to be comfortable with one another in the office. Under the circumstances, though, I don't think now is a wise time to give you the position. That doesn't mean we can't address the situation in the future. I can get along for a while with a temp from an agency, until we see how things work out."

"You would keep the position open?"

His lips kicked up in a half-grin. "No matter what happens between us, I see you as a valuable part of the company. Maybe it's too soon to say this, but I believe you'll come to be more valuable to my heart."

He leaned in, his intention clear. Renee met him halfway, eager to seal their newfound plan with—

"Momma, watch!"

Renee jerked back at Travis's call. Oh, how she'd wanted to place a kiss on Greg's manly, beautiful mouth . . . before being reminded of her son's presence and the fact that she should talk to Travis before showing any physical affection for Greg in front of him.

She turned to see him fly down the slide, as he'd done uncountable times before. "Great, honey bear." She squeezed Greg's hand. "I should take Travis home and get him ready for bed."

"I'll see you Saturday."

She nodded.

Once he walked off, Renee collected Travis and nearly skipped to her apartment. She couldn't wait to call Val to tell her friend she'd been right about Greg.

CHAPTER SIXTEEN

"Come on, Travis. We need to go." Renee knocked on the bathroom door to get her son's attention.

"I don't want to go to first grade." The muffled response sounded suspiciously close to the door, as though he sat with his back against it.

She quelled a groan, unable to blame Travis for his cold feet. Once the excitement of agreeing to a date with Greg had worn off, the nerves began to burn away her enthusiasm, especially after her conversation with Val last night. Odd, she had thought Val would be happy for her. Instead, she received a response that was lukewarm at best. It still ran through her head.

"Hello?" The voice on the other end of the line practically growled the word.

"Hey, Val. You were right."

"About what?"

"Greg and I talked tonight. He is interested in me as more than an employee." She waited for a response that never came, so she added, "I agreed to go out with him."

"That's good."

That was all Val had to say? She'd spouted plenty of advice during other discussions involving Greg. "I'm really nervous about it. Do you think I did the right thing?"

"You worry too much. I'm sure everything will work out for the best, Renee."

The rest of their conversation revolved around nothing more important than the first day of school for the kids. Maybe things were strained at the Sargeant house again, but the up-and-down with Val had begun to exhaust Renee.

At this moment, she had a child to get to school and no time or mental energy to spar with him. "Why don't you want to go to school? You've looked forward to today. It's your first day in the first grade."

And today Renee would see Greg for the first time after their conversation—after he asked her out.

"I changed my mind."

"Well change it again, because you are going to school." *And you are going to face Greg.*

Renee drew in a deep breath to calm her stress and increase her patience. It would do no good to lose her temper. "You'll have fun. Think of all the new things you'll learn and the books you'll read."

"I can get books at the library."

"Steven Travis Burnette, come out of there right now. I don't have time for your games." So much for maintaining a hold on her patience.

Shuffling sounds came from the bathroom, and the door opened a crack, enough to see one of her son's brown eyes. "Why do I have to go to school?"

"Because you're a smart boy, and smart boys know that school is *the* place to become even smarter." Ugh! That wouldn't even convince her. "Are you afraid of something?"

He opened the door all the way. "I'm not afraid of anything."

She crouched to look him in the eyes. "I didn't think so. But if you were, do you know the best way to get over a fear?"

He shook his head.

"It's to march right up to whatever makes you afraid and say, 'You don't scare me, because I have God standing with me.' Do you believe that?" Did she really believe God stood with her through everything, including life as a single mother? It took only a moment to decide that, yes she did.

Then shouldn't she start acting like it?

Travis scrunched up his face in thought and bobbed his head. "I ain't afraid of any ol' school."

Renee pushed up from the floor. "Good boy. Let's go."

A few minutes later, she pulled up in front of the Glenboro Elementary School. Travis gazed at the children filing into the building. He insisted she not get out, that he would go in by himself. As much as she wanted to walk him to class, his hand in hers, she did as he asked.

However, she remained parked at the curb and watched him approach the front doors. He stopped a few feet away, glanced around at the building, the other students, at her. She smiled her encouragement.

Though she couldn't hear him, Travis's lips moved with the words "afraid" and "school." She grinned and mumbled, "That's right. Tell that old school you aren't afraid of it."

And there was no reason for her to be afraid of dating Greg Holmes.

I ain't afraid of any ol' date.

* * *

On her way back from the file room, a quick look at her watch told Renee it was four forty-seven. Thirteen minutes until she would leave to pick up Travis at Mrs. Karrick's apartment and find out how his big day had gone.

She hadn't had time to worry over it or her date with Greg

on Saturday. In fact, she hadn't seen much of her boss, something that brought both relief and disappointment.

As she passed Nora's old office, a deep voice called out, "How was Travis's first day of school?"

Renee skidded to a halt and peeked into the room. Greg was hanging his suit coat on the coat rack. He must have just returned from a late afternoon appointment.

She stepped in as far as the desk in Nora's office—she couldn't stop thinking of it as such—and sighed. "It was a rough start this morning, but I haven't received one of those 'calls to the parent,' so I'm crossing my fingers that all went well."

"That's great." Greg moved behind his desk. "I didn't ask you last night. Where would you like to go Saturday?"

He'd lowered his voice, but not so much that it smacked of a secret or intimate conversation. Renee matched his volume. "Where do you suggest?"

"I know of an Italian restaurant with unbelievable eggplant parmigiana and even better lasagna."

She grinned. "Now, you're making me hungry."

Greg chuckled.

"Sounds perfect."

"Then it's a date."

She walked back into the hallway, unable to contain a smile. Yes, it was a date.

Ahead, Colleen rounded the corner. Thinking the receptionist had continued out front, Renee drew up short at seeing Colleen leaning against the wall across from her desk, eyes wide. "Did I hear right? You and Greg are dating?"

Renee's heart thudded. They had agreed not to keep whatever was between them a secret, yet not purposely announce the news.

"How long has this been going on?"

Renee settled in her chair behind the desk. "It hasn't been 'going on.' We're just having dinner this weekend."

"You'll forgive me if I don't believe you. I saw how he looked at you that night you were at the lanes to bowl."

"Colleen—"

"No wonder he won't let me take Nora's place."

The woman's whine grated on Renee's nerves. "It isn't like that."

"Right."

Colleen stomped off, leaving Renee to shake her head. She waited to feel a twinge of guilt or regret. Oddly, they didn't come.

* * *

Standing in front of the bathroom sink, Renee stared into the mirror at a face that stared back with an expression of stark, raving terror. She closed her eyes, blocking out the image.

Why had she agreed to this night?

Because she *really* liked Greg, both as a boss and a man, and he seemed to like her. They deserved the right to explore a possible future together, didn't they?

Or was she insane?

Of course not. I'm a mature woman—a mother—with a rational mind and a cautious nature.

What if they found they weren't suited for one another?

Easy. We'll go back to being employer and employee as though nothing personal ever happened between us. Mature woman, remember?

Renee opened her eyes and applied lipstick with an unsteady hand, thankful the frosty pink color tinted only her lips and not her skin. She snapped the cap on the tube, picked up her brush, and ran it through her permed waves. The Aqua Net hairspray formed a fog around her face as she sprayed those waves into obedience.

A firm knock on the apartment door—one, two, three raps—froze her in place. She pressed a hand against her tumbling stomach.

"Momma, I think Mr. Greg is here!" Travis shouted the news as though he were twenty feet away rather than four.

"Thank you, honey bear. Get your shoes on."

Renee slid her makeup into a drawer. Though she didn't need to, she adjusted the pastel green polyester blouse she'd tucked into black pleated slacks. Maybe she should change into a dress? All week she'd vacillated between outfits, finally settling on something dressy but not too dressy.

Greg knocked again.

Too late.

She hurried to open the door. "Sorry. I was finishing getting ready."

Her gaze roamed over him. He was handsome anytime, but tonight his looks seemed to take on a special attractiveness. Could it be the pastel blue Polo shirt that highlighted his eyes and hair color? Or was it as simple as the fact that tonight she saw him as a romantic interest rather than a boss?

He smiled. "I don't mind. You look beautiful."

"Thanks. So do you." *Ugh*! Had she just said that to a man? "I mean, you look handsome."

"Hey, Mr. Greg." Travis stood next to Renee, peering up at her date, his greeting saving her from making a bigger fool of herself. "Are you gonna date my momma?"

Renee had purposely avoided using the D-word when asking if he minded her going to out to eat with Mr. Holmes. At the time, he had been ecstatic, again expressing his fondness for Greg.

While she tried to figure out how to answer, Greg crouched in front of her son. "Yes, it is. Is that all right with you?"

Travis shrugged like it was no big deal. "Sure."

Holding her son's hand, Renee drew him away from the door. "Come in. I'll run Travis across the way and be right back."

When she returned, she found Greg sitting on the sofa. She grabbed her purse from the seat of a dining table chair. "Are you ready?"

"If you are."

She locked up, and Greg walked her to the car. He opened the car door for her. "Are you nervous?"

There was no point in denying it. "Honestly? Right now, I'm a bundle of nerves."

"We have something in common, then."

His admission had a calming effect on Renee.

They settled into the car and he pulled out of the apartment complex onto the highway, driving north for a few miles before he asked, "You hadn't told Travis about our date?"

"I didn't hide the fact that we would go out tonight, but I didn't call it a date."

"May I ask why?"

Renee peered out the side window at the passing scenery, the rolling countryside that melded into mountains in the distance. This was a beautiful place to live, even during winter snows.

She shifted in the seat to face Greg. "We said slow and steady, right? Travis is my main consideration. He would love to have a father. He barely remembers his own. But I have to do what is best for him. I've dated a few times since Steve died. Even then, I've tried to protect Travis from thinking that my going out with someone means that man will be around for the long haul."

"I guess I shouldn't have answered his question for you, but once he asked, I felt as though I needed to ask his permission to take you out."

None of the other three men she had gone out with in the past four years had shown such consideration for her son. It melted her concern over any terms they might use to explain tonight. "I understand, and it's fine."

He reached across the seat and took her hand in his. "I've never dated a woman with a child. This is a new experience for me."

"I've never dated my boss. It's a new experience for me, too."

Ten minutes later, Greg held the restaurant door open for Renee to enter. As soon as she stepped inside the dimly lit room with stucco and brick walls straight out of a Tuscan villa, she breathed deep of the aromas. Oregano and basil. Freshly-baked bread. Coffee and tiramisu. "It smells like Italian heaven in here."

"It's one of my favorite restaurants."

A hostess seated them at a private corner table and handed them their menus before weaving back through the tables to the front.

"This is your favorite place to sit?"

"It's my *new* favorite place to sit." The flickering flame of a candle lit his smiling face.

Renee grinned. "You have good taste."

"Once I asked you out, any doubt about my good taste should have been settled."

Oh, this man.

Over dinner—lasagna and ravioli—they talked about everything from her childhood as an Army brat to her marriage and widowhood to his college days playing football at

Appalachian State University and opening Holmes Real Estate Developers. The evening passed in a flash with the laughter good company brings.

They lingered over cannoli, coffee, and prolonged glances until Renee checked her watch and placed her napkin on the table. "We've been gone three hours. I should rescue Mrs. Karrick."

Thirty minutes later, he delivered her to her apartment door and waited until she'd opened it. His gaze slipped to her lips. "Do you mind if I kiss you goodnight?"

She whispered, "Please do."

He leaned forward and cupped the side of her face in a caress that snatched her breath. His lips touched hers, light and warm and a promise of more to come.

He drew back. "Goodnight, Renee."

"G—" She cleared her throat. "Goodnight, Greg. Thank you. I had a wonderful time."

"Then you won't object to doing it again next weekend?"

Was he kidding? "Not at all."

"Good. I'll see you Monday."

He climbed in his car and backed away to wind through the complex and park in a space in front of his own building. Renee watched until he was out of sight, then turned toward Mrs. Karrick's apartment, pulling out her wallet as she approached the door.

A few seconds after she knocked the older woman opened the door. "Hey, Mrs. Karrick. I came to get Travis."

Her son scurried to the door. "We've been playing Candy Land and I won."

"Good for you, honey bear."

Mrs. Karrick laid a hand on Travis's shoulder. "He's a whiz at the game."

Renee glanced at his bare feet. "Grab your shoes and let's go." She pulled some money from her wallet to give to her babysitter.

Mrs. Karrick raised her hands. "Oh, no. I've already been paid."

"What do you mean? I didn't pay you earlier." Had the woman forgotten? After all, she was in her seventies. Maybe Renee should pay more attention to her neighbor's health and memory.

"Your young man paid me before you brought Travis over."

Greg paid her? "He didn't mention it."

"I'd say he's quite a gentleman. Not many of those around these days, not after women started thinking they should do everything themselves. My Barney always opened the door for me, whether it was at the car or entering a building. He'd get put out if I tried to do it myself."

Greg had opened doors for her.

Renee heard her mother's voice whisper in her ear that the man was a keeper. While she and her mother had had their share of clashes over the years, Renee suspected time would prove Momma right. Greg Holmes was indeed a keeper.

CHAPTER SEVENTEEN

Seated behind her desk, pencil in hand, Renee opened the black cover of the day planner on her desk and flipped two pages back to the Saturday she had marked with an asterisk. A tingle shivered through her. The days had flown by since her first date with Greg. They had gone out one other time, not counting the bowling night when she substituted for Debbie, but spoke on the telephone at least every other night after Travis went to bed.

While in the office, they kept their relationship focused on business, though Colleen had made sure everyone knew of their first date. The only one who seemed against it was the receptionist. But surely, everyone saw something special on her face and the way Greg often found a reason to visit her corner to talk.

Her telephone rang. “Renee Burnette.”

“Mrs. Burnette, this is Linda Ferguson from the An Apple a Day Bake-off.”

Renee straightened in her chair. She hadn’t received a call from the organization before. In fact, she still hadn’t settled on a recipe for the competition . . . had given it little thought. “Yes, ma’am?”

“I’m calling to let you know we’ve postponed this Saturday’s event. Unfortunately, there was a small fire in the high school cafeteria.”

“Oh, no.” That must have been the reason for the sirens she

heard this morning. "Was anyone hurt?"

"Thankfully no, and the damage was minimal, but the kitchen won't be available for us to use for two weeks. Our final round will be on September thirteenth. Will you be able to make it?"

Renee checked her calendar again and found no upcoming events that would interfere. In fact, the postponement gave her some breathing room to discover that special recipe. "Yes. That's fine."

"Good. Another entrant has had to pull out, but we'll look forward to seeing you on the thirteenth."

Renee hung up the phone and wrote the contest on the calendar. Not that she'd need the reminder.

The withdrawal of a contestant left her competing against Val and one other woman. Somehow, when there were three competitors, it hadn't seemed as delicate a tightrope to walk. Now, it felt as though she would compete against Val alone.

No matter who baked alongside her that Saturday, it was time to buckle down and decide on a recipe.

* * *

Sitting at her desk, Renee covered a yawn. She had stayed up baking until almost twelve-thirty. The news yesterday of a reprieve due to the fire didn't mean she could delay finding the perfect recipe for the final round of the bake-off.

She entered the office kitchen to pour herself a cup of coffee, even though it was after one-thirty. At the sound of rustling and footsteps, she looked up to find Greg entering the room. Her smile voluntarily spread. He didn't call her last night as he usually did, and today, their paths hadn't crossed until now. Come to think of it, they hadn't spoken since yesterday morning.

"How has your day gone?"

"I've had better." He grabbed a Styrofoam cup, filled it, and turned to go—all without saying another word to her.

The clipped response and tight mouth took Renee aback. "Is something wrong with the new development?"

"It's fine. I need to get to work, Renee." He raised an eyebrow, his look saying she did, too.

She shivered with the chill emanating from his cold shoulder. *What on earth caused that black frame of mind?*

The temp secretary the agency had sent remained away from the office for the afternoon with already scheduled doctors' appointments. Greg called Renee in twice to dictate letters but acted as though he barely knew she was there. He didn't smile or ask how her day was going. He didn't joke about the bitter coffee in the break room or look at her with that "I can't wait to talk after work" expression.

No, that wasn't quite true. Off and on, he glanced at her and opened his mouth, only to close it again and scowl. For the life of her, she couldn't figure out what was wrong with Greg, and he wasn't sharing.

Renee cleaned off the top of her desk, ready to get the frustrating afternoon behind her and pick up Travis from her neighbor. Her phone buzzed, and she picked up the receiver. "Renee Burnette."

"Could you come in here, please?"

Not again. "Yes, sir."

Renee pulled her steno pad and a pen from the desk drawer and entered Greg's office. The lines on his face still hadn't relaxed. In fact, he looked more agitated than earlier.

"Close the door, please."

So stiff. So polite. But a black cloud hung over his head. After sitting in the chair across the desk from him, she opened the pad and waited.

"You won't need that."

Something was terribly wrong.

"Renee, I've put this off for as long as possible. I'll start by admitting I've enjoyed our time together outside of work the past two weeks."

Then why didn't it sound like it? "But?"

"From now on, I think we should stick to a business relationship."

The air around her grew stifling, almost as though she breathed in that black cloud. A lump formed in her chest, pressing on her lungs. He was breaking up with her? Already?

"I don't want to be unfair to you and let you continue thinking things will work out between us. It's best to end our personal relationship before either of us gets too involved."

Her heart thudded in her ears like a basketball dribbled on a court. *Too late.*

Renee swallowed and blinked fast to control the moisture building in her eyes. She remained silent until she felt she could speak in a voice that didn't shriek or croak. "Is this because of what Travis said on Sunday? He's a little boy. He doesn't understand." During another ice cream outing, Travis had blurted out a wish for her and Greg to marry, so the two "men" could toss a baseball in that lovely new yard.

"This has nothing to do with Travis. He's a great kid."

But she wasn't a great girlfriend? "Can you at least tell me what I did to upset you?"

Greg picked up a pen, leaned back in his chair, and rolled the instrument between his palms. He tried to display an outer show of calm, but Renee judged the tick at his mouth as anxiety. "Let's just say you and I want a different kind of relationship."

A different kind of relationship? She could only think of one meaning to that statement. Yes, they had kissed, but up to now, he'd acted like a gentleman. A keeper. How he'd had her fooled.

"We agreed that if it didn't work out, we would act like adults and go on about our business. I told you before that you're a valuable part of the company, Renee. That hasn't changed."

He thought they could go on as before? They had agreed, but as of this moment, she didn't see how it would work. "So, we'll ignore the past two weeks?"

Greg flinched. "It's for the best."

With as much dignity as she could muster, she stood and forced a blithe attitude into her voice. "Then if that was all you wanted from me, I'll see you tomorrow."

Greg stared at her as though he'd expected something else—an argument or tears? He gathered himself and acknowledged her statement with a quick and fierce bob of dismissal. Before she reached the door and looked back, he had lowered his gaze to read the correspondence on his desk.

Renee held her head high as she walked out of his office. She studied Nora's old space—the furniture, the prints on the walls, the large desk. He had promised to hold Nora's position until they saw how things would go between them. Well, she could kiss that opportunity goodbye, too.

With his rejection of her, she didn't even care.

At her desk, she tossed the notepad and pen back into the drawer, grabbed her purse, and shut off the lights. Ignoring Debbie's call of "Goodnight," Renee slipped out the back door of the building. By the time she reached her car, she could barely see to slide the key into the door lock as tears filled her eyes.

. . . we would act like adults and go on about our business.

She didn't feel much like an adult at the moment. She felt more like that lonely little girl who too often found herself without a friend.

Renee dug into her purse for a tissue and wiped away the moisture on her face. *This. This* was why she didn't want to get involved in an office romance. This was why she had kept her feelings for Greg to herself for weeks.

Well, she had learned her lesson. *Never fall in love with your boss or anyone else you'd be forced to see every day.*

She could hold her breath and hope until she was blue in the face that her blunder wouldn't cost her a job she enjoyed. She hoped it wouldn't cost her—and her son—the chance to move out of their nothing little apartment.

Most of all, she hoped her heart would heal.

CHAPTER EIGHTEEN

"I've done a horrible thing."

Standing at the kitchen counter, Renee pulled the phone's receiver away from her ear and frowned at it. After these past twenty-four hours, ever since Greg decided to drop her, she had no patience to listen to whatever silly thing Val had done to get her husband's back up this time.

Thankfully, her boss had been out of the office today and would be gone the rest of the week—a last-minute trip out of town, he said—so she would have a reprieve from walking on eggshells around him.

With a soft sigh, she placed the phone against her ear again. Last night, she cried over the phone to Val about the breakup, so it was only fair to listen to whatever troubled her tonight. "I'm sure it wasn't that bad."

"No, it was worse, and you're going to hate me for it."

That got Renee's attention. "Why would I hate you?" With the silence on the other end, Renee thought Val had hung up on her. "Hello?"

"I saw Greg during lunch on Monday at Gully's. I told him how much you loved his house and the idea of getting the promotion you'd wanted." The words poured with the speed of water through the break in a dam. "I'm so ashamed of myself."

Why would she be ashamed? "It's all right. Greg knew I liked his new place and we agreed the timing wasn't right with the promotion."

"You d-don't understand." Val's sobs on the other end of the line tore at Renee's heart. "I-I told Greg that you only . . ."

Renee attempted to make sense of what her friend tried to tell her. "That I only what?" As the question left her mouth, a horrible thought entered her mind, so horrible she couldn't believe it might be true. She gripped the receiver like it was a rope—the only thing to save her from washing over the edge of Val's verbal dam. "Please don't say you told Greg I was only interested in him because of the promotion and his new house."

"Before I could stop myself, the words tumbled out of my mouth."

Renee gripped the phone tighter. "You mean the lie tumbled out!" No wonder he broke up with her.

Memories flooded her mind. Memories of Greg's encouragement during the bake-off. The day he showed her the house. Their dates . . . as few of them as there were.

Let's just say you and I want a different kind of relationship.

Guilt wiggled into her mind. She hadn't sought an explanation from Greg about what he meant by the statement, assuming she knew. Now, she realized she'd misunderstood.

"What's wrong, Momma?"

Renee covered the receiver. She attempted to smile but the movement only reminded her of the tick alongside Greg's mouth yesterday. "Finish your supper, Travis."

She fought the desire to hang up on Val, sending a message the woman couldn't mistake.

"I . . ." The word came out of Val like a hushed breath, and Renee wasn't sure she actually heard it. Val sniffled. "I'm so sorry. I've never done anything this awful in my life. I couldn't sleep last night after you told me about the breakup, knowing it was my fault. Poor Pete." *Sniff.* "I've cried on his shoulder all day."

Poor Pete? What about poor Renee?

She hardened her heart against the misery in Val's voice and the apology that hid somewhere in those self-absorbed words. With one slash of her tongue, the woman had sabotaged whatever future Renee might have with Greg, along with their friendship.

"I'll call Greg and make sure he understands that I . . . that I lied, and you're only interested in him."

"You've done enough. I'll handle my relationship with my boss from now on." How she didn't know. She didn't even know if she cared to work things out with Greg after he dumped her so easily. She thought they had moved toward something special. But she might as well be a total stranger to him if he willingly thought of her as callous and conniving.

Renee scrubbed a hand down her face, still trying to comprehend the fact that Val had betrayed her. "Why would you do something like that, Val? I thought we were friends . . . best friends."

And here Renee imagined that, for most of her life, she had missed out when it came to having close relationships with other women. It seemed the only thing she missed out on was the heart-wrenching drama.

"We are best friends, Renee. At least, I hope we can stay that way."

"Then help me to understand why you did what you did. Why have you treated me this way?"

It seemed like forever waiting for Val to speak again, but Renee refused to hang up without an answer.

"Pete and I had a massive argument Sunday. Then when I found out that another competitor had to bow out of the bake-off, leaving only three of us, I . . . I panicked. I got scared you would win, so I figured if your mind was on something else . . ."

"My mind wouldn't be focused on finding a winning recipe. Maybe I'd drop out, too?"

"Yes."

"What happened to the friendly rivalry you talked about?" Renee closed her eyes and breathed in, breathed out. She tried to calm the storm of temper that rose inside her. "Val, I never wished to compete against you. I offered to work with you to save our friendship, but you said no and, in the end, chose to throw it away."

"I know. Now I wish with everything in me I'd said yes to you." A heavy sigh came across the line. "Pete lost his job."

Renee stilled at Val's quiet statement. "What? When?"

"The day we were supposed to go to the event at his work. Pete suspected it was coming but never told me. It's why he's been so concerned about our financial s-situation."

The sob on the other end softened that heart Renee had hardened. "I'm sorry."

"I thought winning the money from the bake-off would tide us over for a while and keep Pete and me from fighting so much." Another sniffle. "But it's no excuse for what I did to you."

"Val, I'm not your only competition. There's another woman in the final round. How can you be sure you will win over her?"

"I can't, but you scored highest in the last round, and I know what a good baker you are. I figured you would provide the biggest challenge."

She had scored highest of the eleven competitors with her Bougatsa? "How did you find that out?"

"I sneaked a peek at the score sheet when I picked up my dish."

Greg never mentioned it. Then again, maybe he wasn't given the actual scores. "It doesn't mean what I bake will bring the same result next time."

"I know. I haven't been thinking straight lately."

Or at all.

"You could have told me about Pete's job."

"It wasn't news we were eager to spread around. Pride got in our way. Maybe some guilt. Neither of us had much in the way of material things growing up, so we've enjoyed spending money."

"I guess I can understand that." What she didn't understand was why Val felt she had to ruin Renee's life, too.

"I've asked God to forgive me for my deception. Will you forgive me?"

Could she?

Renee's gaze slipped to the dining table that still held a number of cookbooks, including the one with the mustard-colored cover and red lettering.

Two are better than one.

"Remember that cookbook I bought a couple of months ago? *Mrs. Canfield's Cookery Book*?"

Sniffle. "Yes."

"Besides recipes, it's loaded with wisdom and scripture. These words from Ecclesiastes struck me as particularly wise, because it describes what I've hoped to experience from the friendships in my life: 'Two are better than one, because they have a good reward for their labor: for if they fall, the one will lift up his fellow—"

"'But woe to him that is alone when he falleth, for he hath not another to help him up.'" Val finished the verse for her. The sobbing intensified. "I should have talked to you. I should have been honest. It's what people do when they care about each other."

"I would have tried my best to lift you up."

Lord, help me to know what to do.

An unexpected peace settled over Renee. "It isn't too late for me to try, Val. Tell me how to lift you up."

"Y-You already have by asking."

* * *

"Momma, I want to go to the playground."

"Not now, Travis. I have baking to do."

"You always have baking to do."

Renee rubbed her forehead. "This is important. We'll do something together later, okay? For now, just watch TV or something."

She ignored whatever he mumbled in response and opened the cabinet door where she kept her spices and baking ingredients. She studied the shelves, moving this bottle and that container. There must be something here that would give her an idea for her entry in the final round of the bake-off.

Seeing the sage, her forehead crimped. What about an apple stuffing? She hung her head in frustration. One of the contestants had entered that in the last round.

Apple pie with . . . What?

Apple dumplings?

Apple strudel?

Apple chili? A burst of laughter bubbled up. Now, she'd hit the height of ridiculousness. Unless . . . No.

Renee had to face it. After all she had experienced lately and Val's announcement about Pete's job loss, inspiration played hide and seek with her.

A shout outside her apartment caught her attention. She

shut the pantry door and peered out the window. Unable to see anyone from that angle, but still hearing strained voices, she opened the door and stepped outside. At the curb, Greg crouched in front of Travis, his hands clutching her child's arms.

Travis? What was he doing out here? He should be inside watching television. How had she missed him leaving the apartment? And why was Greg holding on to her son like that?

Heart racing, Renee tried to shove aside a growing panic and rushed down the sidewalk. "What's going on?" Her son turned his head to look at her, tears tracking down his face. "Oh, honey bear, what happened? Are you hurt? What are you doing outside?" Had Greg hurt her boy? Her breath stalled. Surely not.

"He's fine, Renee." Greg let go of Travis and pushed to his feet. "But it was a close call."

She pulled Travis into a possessive hug, her hand resting on the top of her son's head. "A close call? What happened?"

"He ran between parked cars. A driver approached. He wouldn't have seen Travis in time to stop."

All the air seeped out of Renee's lungs and her head felt light. *No! Stop!* The shout she had heard a couple of minutes ago finally sank in. "You stopped him in time?" *You saved him?*

"I think I scared him when I grabbed hold of his arm, but I couldn't let him keep going." He reached out as though he'd ruffle Travis's hair, but with her hand there, his arm veered off and his fingers squeezed her son's shoulder in a way that appeared half-reassuring and half-apologetic.

Renee swallowed the tingle in her throat. "I don't know how to thank you."

"No need."

She knelt in front of Travis, her gaze glued to his. "I thought you were inside."

"I told you I wanted to go to the playground."

"Honey, I said we'd do it later."

"It's always later, Momma. You don't do anything with me anymore. All you want to do is bake things."

Her body temperature rose with the truth in his words and the embarrassment of hearing them spoken in someone else's presence—in Greg's presence. She dared a glance up at her boss—her short-time boyfriend—seeing what could only be pity in his eyes.

Travis pulled away from her. "I hate apples!"

Me, too. Renee wished she'd never heard of the An Apple A Day Bake-off. "The contest will be over soon. Things will get back to normal." But would they really?

Mrs. Karrick stepped out of her apartment and stopped beside Travis. Her gray eyebrows were drawn into a vee. "I heard a shout. Is everything all right?"

Renee flashed a pained smile. "It's fine now. Thanks to Mr. Holmes."

The woman looked from Renee to Greg and back to Renee. "I froze some grape Kool-Aid earlier. If it's okay with you, I can take Travis in for a popsicle."

Travis perked up. "Can I have one?" At the mention of a treat, he seemed to have put the close call with a car out of his mind.

Grateful for Mrs. Karrick's offer, Renee wiped the tear tracks from her son's face, dampening her thumbs. "Sure. I'll come get you in a few minutes." She tipped his chin up. "Then we'll talk."

Travis pulled away from her hold. "Yes, ma'am."

She shuddered at the memory of those screeching tires and Greg's warning shout. She'd almost lost Travis due to her lack of attention to her own son.

Once they disappeared behind the neighbor's door, leaving

her alone with Greg, she turned to face him—to face more of his disappointment in her. She rubbed her arms as though the outside temperature had dipped to fifty degrees. "I don't know what to say, other than to thank you for what you did."

"Anyone would have—"

"I don't want you to think I'm a horrible mother." The words tumbled out.

"You're not a horrible mother, Renee. Things happen. Kids are quick-escape artists."

Now that he was here, should she bring up Val's lie? A voice inside urged her to vindicate herself. But that meant placing her friend in a poor light, and she could hear her grandmother's admonishment that two wrongs didn't make a right. Besides, she could never lift Val up as she had promised to do by dragging her down in the eyes of someone else.

Why bother with a defense, anyway? Brushing her aside so easily proved Greg didn't care enough to want to believe her.

The two of them stood on the sidewalk, an awkward silence filling the autumn air until she couldn't stand it anymore. "Thanks again."

Renee's quick, barefoot steps rushed her toward Mrs. Karrick's door. She pretended she hadn't heard Greg call her name, too embarrassed and too heartbroken right now to deal with whatever he wanted to say.

CHAPTER NINETEEN

Renee closed the bedroom door, leaving Travis to sleep in her bed. She slumped in her seat at the dining table and tilted her head back to stare at the popcorn ceiling. The final round of the bake-off was in two days, and she couldn't summon any interest in finding a recipe that would see her depositing that check for $1,500 into her bank account. If she didn't find something soon, all she'd have accomplished these past two months would have amounted to nothing.

Maybe not quite nothing. If her recent experiences had taught Renee one thing, it was that she was tired. Tired of the striving, of the fighting, of the giving of herself in futile attempts to prove her competency and gain an elusive dream.

She was tired of the struggle to be the perfect mom, the perfect employee and co-worker, the perfect friend, and the perfect Christian. Because she had failed at every turn.

Travis grew increasingly rebellious and antagonistic toward her baking.

Greg barely talked to her unless it pertained to her job. Oddly, though, since Travis's near accident, his icy gaze had thawed—drip by drip. He no longer looked at her as though she was a modern-day Jezebel.

But their time together at the office tortured her. Greg might consider her a satisfactory employee, but he no longer considered her worthy of loving. No matter what he said after saving Travis, he must also consider her a poor excuse for a mother for letting her obsession with a baking competition get in the way of her son's safety.

Renee's friendship with Val had teetered on the edge of crumbling. It remained fragile as they worked through their differences. One day, she hoped they would restore the depth of their relationship, but for now, Renee still struggled to fully forgive Val.

And her reliance on God? Renee covered her face with her hands, as though that could hide her inadequacies from the One who knew every inch of her inside and out—every thought and ambition and desire. Every insecure little cell in her body.

She couldn't hide from God the fact that what Val told Greg was true—to a degree. She had desired the position as his secretary. She had coveted his house and experienced an envy that ate at her. Even though she never went through with the idea, the thought of playing up to him to gain Nora's job *had* entered her mind.

Had she subconsciously attached herself to Greg for selfish reasons? Had she convinced herself of her feelings for him to gain the things she desired? If she could turn back time, could she be satisfied in this tiny apartment and in her position as Jim and Dave's secretary if it meant renewing that personal relationship with Greg?

The tears that gathered like flood waters in her eyes streaked down her face, then dripped off her jaw onto the surface of the table. Yes. Yes, she could. That walking-on-the-edge-of-love emotion was real.

She palmed away the wetness from her cheeks and closed her eyes. "God, I don't know what to do. What good is owning a house if it doesn't hold a loving family? What good is staying in one place if I have no close friends?"

Picking up an apple from the basket on the table, she turned it over in her hands, seeing the wormhole she hadn't noticed when buying it. Rather than appreciate the sweet fruit of her childhood, over the years, she'd let discontentment bore through her joy like the worm through this apple. Why? Had her childhood been so bad?

Her parents loved her and, as she tried to do for Travis, they had provided for her the best they knew how given the nature of her father's career. Although Dad could be autocratic, she had never gone without necessities and his care.

Friends often envied her for having experienced different cultures while living in various parts of the country and world. She'd learned to speak German during the months her father was stationed in that country, and much of the language still stuck with her. She had visited European monuments daily that people paid good travel money to see. Some people would say she'd been blessed. At the time, she had believed the nomadic life to be a curse.

"What good am I to You, Lord, if in my discontent, I dismiss the blessings You've graced me with in life?"

Compelled to occupy her mind with something other than "woe-is-me" thoughts, she pulled a cookbook—*Mrs. Canfield's Cookery Book*—toward her and turned the pages with the speed of an anemic slug, barely seeing the titles of the recipes.

Then her gaze lit on the Henry David Thoreau quote she'd read the day she bought the book: *Friends...they cherish one another's hopes. They are kind to one another's dreams.*

Renee had expected Val to honor and cherish her dreams without giving any thought to Val's dreams for the prize money. To her, it had seemed Val only saw the winnings as more money to spend on things she wanted, when Renee had a better plan for the money.

Even if she were to win the bake-off, how could she enjoy the victory? How could she appreciate a new place to live knowing the Sargeants needed the money more? Now that she knew the reason for Val's desire to win, she would be greedy to ignore her friend's situation. How did she cherish Val's hope?

"What would You have me do?"

When the idea came to her, she tried to brush it away before letting it take root. But ideas were stubborn, especially when they were an answer to prayer.

Renee shut the cookbook and rose from her seat. She'd handle the situation first thing tomorrow morning.

* * *

The bottoms of Renee's walking shoes skimmed the earth with a light touch each time the playground swing swayed forward and glided back. Right now, she should be in the high school cafeteria baking her third dish for the An Apple a Day Bake-off. Instead, she was seated on hard plastic and holding tight to two chains while earth changed to sky and sky back to earth.

The constant back and forth felt like a metaphor for her life. Never steady. Never still. Always taking steps forward to find herself moving backward. All the while, a steady breeze of self-doubt rose to blow against her face.

But she hadn't really stepped back this time, because if that were the case, she wouldn't have this peace in her soul that she'd done the right thing.

Renee had considered going to the event to support Val and prove there were no hard feelings, but Greg would be there, and she couldn't face him today, not in that environment. She found it hard enough at work, though she had begun to accept the finality of their time together outside the office. It helped that, with his move, she would no longer see him around the apartment complex.

"Watch me, Momma."

Travis grabbed a metal bar on the merry-go-round and pushed it, running until he could hop on and ride while the playground piece spun in circles. When the merry-go-round slowed, she dragged a foot to stop the swing and walked over to her son. "Would you like me to push you?"

"Yeah!"

"Okay, hold on." She gave the ride a few shoves, sending it into enough of a spin to please her son but not make him sick or scared from the whirl.

"Renee?"

She whipped around, her eyes wide. "What are you doing here, Val? Shouldn't you be at the bake-off?"

Val stopped about ten feet away, a wary look on her face, as though she thought Renee might bite. "With only two of us, it didn't take long. I wish you hadn't dropped out."

Renee's eyebrows rose in a "Really?" expression.

"I know. Ironic."

Renee shrugged, not wishing to rehash their issue. "It was for the best."

"Do you have a few minutes to talk?"

They had spoken on the phone once or twice since Val's confession but hadn't seen one another in person, not even in church, and Val had skipped the last Culinary Capers meeting.

Renee turned to Travis. "Go ahead and play while Mrs. Sargeant and I talk."

"Okay." He jumped off the slowing merry-go-round and headed for the slide at a run.

Renee joined Val, positioning herself in a way that allowed her to keep an eye on her son. "How did you know where to find me?"

"I saw Mrs. Karrick sitting outside."

That made sense. As they left the apartment thirty minutes ago, Renee had stopped to say hello to the woman. In their short discussion, she had mentioned taking Travis to the playground.

Renee drew up her courage to ask the question dying to pass her lips. "How did you do?"

A spark lit Val's eyes. "I won."

Even though she had known it was likely to happen, the words took Renee aback with a momentary envy, or maybe worse, jealousy. She feared she'd have to push the proper—the expected—declaration from her mouth. But the negative emotion faded and the words came out, accompanied by a smile. "Congratulations. That's great."

Val reached into her purse and pulled out a check. "I want you to have this."

Before she could talk herself out of it, Renee reached for the paper, her fingers falling short of snatching it. Fifteen hundred dollars? Val was giving the prize money to her?

She pushed Val's hand away. "I can't take this. I wasn't even there."

"Yes, you can, because I don't want it, Renee." Val shoved the check into Renee's hand, then took a step back and raised her hands to ward off the attempt to return the money. "Besides, it's made out to you, so it won't do me any good."

Sure enough. The check had her name on it. "Why would you do this?"

"Even after our conversation, I couldn't sleep or eat, knowing what I'd done to you, that it was because of me that you and Greg split. Then you quit the bake-off. You sacrificed your dream for me and for my family. I didn't deserve to win." Val's lips curved upward. "After a lot of prayer and discussion with Pete, the idea of giving you the prize money—should I win, of course—brought me the peace I needed."

Renee shook her head. "I still can't take it. You need that money right now."

"I don't need it any more than you do . . . probably less."

Two children ran past them onto the playground. Renee checked on Travis and found him laughing with the little girl who had fallen off the slide a few weeks ago. He was happy and occupied, so she returned to the conversation, still holding out the check. A part of her wanted to keep it as though she had earned it for all she'd been through. "Here. Have them issue a new one in your name." *Take it before I change my mind.*

"I'm guessing you weren't at the bake-off today because of Greg." Val bit her lip but ignored the check. "You told me not to say anything, but I couldn't let him continue to think of you in a bad light because of me."

Renee closed her eyes and released a groan. "Oh, Val."

"It's okay."

Val's next words were mumbled, but Renee caught the gist of them. "You told him you lied about my motive for dating him?"

"No. Not at first. He didn't let me. To be honest, I think he was already kicking himself for trusting in my words rather than trusting in the person he knew."

So, he's wishy-washy and gullible. Great.

Renee crossed her arms. "Well, it's too late. I can't continue to work for him. It's too awkward. I've already decided that on Monday I'll resign."

"Renee, please don't do something you'll regret. He truly likes you. That hasn't changed. You should have seen him MC the bake-off. Before he's been upbeat and amusing. Today, he was serious and looked despondent. I know it was because you weren't there. Everyone saw it and people were talking about it. That's why I knew I had to go against your wishes and say something. You two should be together. But before I could tell him I'd lied, Renee, Greg told me he'd thought over what I'd said and didn't believe me. He regrets how he treated you. Isn't that wonderful?"

Could Val be right? Was Greg sorry for thinking the worst about her? Since his return to the office after saving Travis, she had caught him looking at her with an expression she hadn't dared to believe was regret. But what did that mean in the long term? Would he always be quick to see her in a negative light and cast her aside as if she weren't good enough? She stared at the ground, but the grass didn't hold the answers to her questions.

"There's something else you should know."

Renee cocked her head and studied Val to get a hint as to the topic, not sure she could absorb any further news—good or bad.

"Pete may have found a job. It isn't final yet, but if it works out, we'll sell the house and move to South Carolina."

"No." Renee's arms dropped to her sides. "I mean . . . I'm glad for the job, but . . ." It was happening again. She made a friend only to have to say goodbye. Only this time, Renee was the one staying, while her friend left.

"We'll only live an hour away, so we'll still get together."

But with both of them having busy lives, how often would that be?

Val grasped her hand. "I haven't always shown it, but our friendship is too important to me to let a few miles get in the way."

Renee swallowed the lump in her throat. "To me, too."

"I need to go, but I'll see you soon."

After Val left, Renee glanced down at her hand. She still held the check.

* * *

That night, Renee dried the last of the supper pans and put them in the cabinet, taking care to not rattle the pots and wake up Travis in his bed. A quiet rap on the door caught her attention.

She tossed the dishtowel on the counter and hurried to answer, swinging the door open to find the last person she expected to see. "Greg." After her conversation with Val, she could guess what brought him here, but not what would come of it.

Hands stuffed in the pockets of his jeans and shoulders hunched, he gave her a shy smile. "Hi, Renee. I hope it isn't too late for a visit."

"Well, I . . ." She glanced back at Travis.

Greg peered over her shoulder into the apartment. "Maybe we could talk out here?"

Renee nodded and stepped outside, pulling the door closed behind her. She folded her arms across her chest and waited.

His gaze bounced to the concrete and back to her. "I missed seeing you at the bake-off today. Your friend Val said you withdrew a couple of days ago."

"I did."

"Val seemed to think you did it for her."

Renee's face warmed, visibly acknowledging his statement. The subject of the bake-off brought to mind the check and her indecision over what to do with it.

A grin broke out on Greg's face. "That was an unselfish act, Renee."

Rather than accept the comment at face value, her hackles rose. "I can be unselfish."

He grimaced. "I didn't mean it like that."

"Then what did you mean?"

"Just that I was an idiot to believe with my head what my heart told me was a lie."

The admission didn't satisfy. "One minute I'm a conniving and manipulative woman, and the next I'm not?" It was her turn to grimace. He was trying to apologize . . . maybe, and she was provoking him.

"You were never conniving and manipulative. I accused you of something and pronounced a sentence without asking for the truth. I'm sorry."

"Why would you have believed Val?"

"She was your friend. She knew you." He released a heavy breath. "No, it was more than that. I dated a woman once and almost married her. Then I found out she'd been deceiving me all along. I guess I let my past hurt feelings speak for me. When I left Gully's, I kept thinking about that day at the house. There was such a dreamy look on your face as you went through each room. Before that day, you seemed to—I don't know—run from me."

"I didn't ask to see the house."

"You're right. Yet after talking to Val, a voice in my head said I'd been foolish to show it to you before knowing how you felt about me. Then, I imagined I'd been maneuvered into offering to wait to fill Nora's job until we saw where things would go between us."

"I never meant for you to feel that way. I intended to speak up weeks ago about the position, but the time never seemed right, and asking for something I want is not natural for me." But it may be time to change that. "You weren't totally wrong about me. I did want the position, and I was envious of your ability to move into that beautiful house. It even crossed my mind to flirt with you. I rejected the idea right away, because it isn't me, Greg. But I'm sorry it even popped into my mind."

"It took several days of soul-searching at my grandparents' farm and the recollection of our conversation that day on the playground. Recalling your honesty that day and concern over Travis made me realize how wrong I was." He reached out and took her hand, his thumb running over her skin. "I haven't known how to fix things. Is it possible for us to start over?"

She studied the vulnerable look, a look she had never seen on his face before. He was always so confident.

Honestly? She had forgiven him the moment he showed up on her doorstep with that hangdog look on his face. "I think we had better. I'm tired of being miserable, and that little boy in there misses you."

"I've missed him, too." Greg dropped his hand. "One more thing."

"What?"

"No more temp secretaries, okay? I want you in Nora's office Monday morning. Colleen can move into your spot, and we'll find a new receptionist."

A momentary fear gripped her. What if her co-workers assumed she had used Greg to get Nora's job, just as he had done?

"I see those wheels turning, Renee, and I don't care what others in the office think."

She relaxed. She and Greg knew the truth. God knew the truth. No one else mattered. "Deal."

He looked at the hand she held out for him to shake, then slipped his arms around her and lowered his lips until they hovered near hers. "This is how we seal our agreement."

Goodness. She'd have to think of more agreements for them to make.

Love. Friendship. Family. God was stirring together the

ingredients for a winning future, and Renee couldn't wait to see how it turned out.

EPILOGUE

March 1987

Greg and Pete, one on each end, hoisted the sofa bed where Travis had slept for so long. They tipped it this way and that, maneuvering it through the apartment doorway without scraping the door frame. A heroic feat.

Renee peered out the window, watching them carry it to the trailer Greg had rented. She closed the blind and eyed the empty space on the wall. The living area in the apartment looked so much larger with the sofa gone.

She glanced toward the kitchen, the counter clean and clear of everything that had previously occupied it. That room still looked tiny, and when she compared it in her mind to the kitchen in Greg's—her—new house, it shrank even more.

Was this really happening? Was she newly married to a fantastic guy and moving out of this small space into a home with room for four of these apartments?

"Hey, Renee, what do you want to do with the clothes in the closet?"

"There's an empty box on the bed, Val." Renee entered the bedroom to join her friend in finishing the packing. She and Greg hoped to move everything this morning, to give them time this afternoon to pick up Travis from his grandparents and unpack the essentials. "I appreciate you and Pete coming today to help."

"That's what friends are for. Besides, you and Greg helped us when we moved, and we had three times as much stuff as you." Val took a blouse from Renee's closet, folded it, and placed it in a box on the bed. "I can't believe we're already helping you move out of this place. It seems like you and Greg only started dating last week."

"It's been six months. Six . . . long . . . months." Renee laughed. "And a glorious honeymoon."

"I don't mean to beat a dead horse, but I feel so fortunate that you—"

"Don't say it, Val. What happened last year is old news. We got past it and our friendship has come through stronger for it." Renee had come through it stronger.

"I know." Val reached an arm around her and squeezed. "You're my best friend and always will be."

"Through rain or shine."

"Through rain or shine."

Months ago, Renee had talked it over with Greg, then Val. They all decided the prize money for the bake-off should go to the food pantry in town. It was strange how unearned money was never missed.

Renee wiped the moisture away from under her eyes and walked out of the bedroom. "Will we have enough room in the trailer, honey?"

"Between it and the cars, we're good." Greg grunted as he lifted one of the last of the boxes to carry to the car. "What do you have in here?"

She studied the box. "Books, mostly. I'm afraid that bookshelf in the den won't remain empty for long. Of course, most of my cookbooks, which are in the box on the counter, will go on a shelf in the kitchen."

"It's a good thing I'm not a big reader. Fill the shelves to your heart's content." He shifted the box in his arms as he tried to open the apartment door.

"Here, let me get it." Renee opened the door, then lifted to her toes and planted a kiss on his cheek. "You're a good sport."

"No, I'm a thoroughly love-struck man." He winked and walked out the door to add the box to the back seat of her car.

An hour later, once everything else had been loaded and Pete and Val were on their way to the Holmes house in Mountain Hollow, only one box of books remained. For some reason, Renee felt pressed to complete a task before closing that box.

Greg walked back into the apartment. "Are you ready, Renee?"

"In a moment, sweetheart."

She pulled *Mrs. Canfield's Cookery Book* from the top of the box, set it on the kitchen counter, and turned to the section that held sayings about friendship. With pen in hand, she printed under the last words *How good and pleasant it is when God's people live together in unity! Psalm 133:1.* There. She'd inserted something of herself into the book that held the added wisdom and cooking expertise of others throughout the past seven-plus decades.

Already, she knew she wouldn't keep the cookbook. After all, its wisdom had helped her through a rough patch, and she suspected it could help someone else.

Renee shut the book and put it back on top of the box Greg held, then she wrapped her arms around his neck and kissed his lips, lingering long enough to hear his soft groan. "Now, I'm ready."

After one last look at the empty apartment, Renee followed her new husband out the door and into their future together.

What a pleasure it has been to work with my marvelous fellow authors to bring you the Apron Strings series. My special thanks to Jenny Knipfer for coming up with the idea and Dawn Kinzer for inviting me to take part. But it has truly been a group effort. And speaking of groups . . .

I'm thrilled to have gotten to interact with readers through our Facebook Apron Strings Readers Group. Though we all participated I want to give a special shout out to Amy Walsh for taking the lead and Patti Wolf for her fun videos. Thank you to those who conversed with us and eagerly awaited the book releases. Readers make writing both enjoyable and worthwhile.

I want to thank author Heidi Chiavaroli for her spot-on insight into the story. I've depended on her advice for well over a decade, and I'm a better writer for it.

Again, valued reader, if you enjoyed this story in the Apron Strings series, please show *Renee* some review love so others can decide if they, too, might enjoy it. A couple of lines of what you did or didn't like is all it takes.

Happy reading!

Enjoy the following recipes!

Apple Slices

My grandmother made this dessert. Even though I'm not much of a baker, I'm so thankful I asked her for the recipe.

Crust:
3 cups flour
½ teaspoon salt
1 cup shortening
½ cup milk
1 egg yolk (save the egg white to brush over the top)

Filling:
6 cups sliced apples
1 ½ cups sugar
2 tablespoons flour
½ teaspoon cinnamon
¼ cup margarine
(Optional: raisins)

Glaze:
½ to 1 cup powdered sugar
2 to 3 tablespoons milk
1/8 teaspoon vanilla

Preheat the oven to 350º. Mix the ingredients for the crust and divide the dough in half. Roll out one of the dough halves and lay it in a jelly roll pan. In a bowl, mix the apples, sugar, flour, cinnamon, and margarine and spoon over the bottom crust. Roll out the second half of the dough and lay over the top. Brush the top with the egg white and bake for 45 minutes. After baking, mix the glaze ingredients and pour over the crust while it's still warm, then cut the dessert in squares.

Violet's Apple Cake

(Updated Version of a 19th Century Recipe)

Years ago, when my first book released, *The Yuletide Angel*, I shared this recipe I'd found in a 19th-century cookbook.

2 cups Granny Smith apples, peeled and diced (about two apples)
3 cups brown sugar

Cook the apples in brown sugar on low until the apples begin to become clear (about thirty minutes, so do this early), then let the mixture cool completely.

Cake Batter:
1 cup sugar
½ cup butter (one stick)
4 cups flour
2 eggs
1 cup sour milk (add 1 tablespoon lemon juice to enough milk to make one cup – let sit five minutes)
1 teaspoon baking soda
2 teaspoons cinnamon
½ teaspoon ground cloves
½ teaspoon nutmeg

Preheat the oven to 350°. Add the cooled apples and brown sugar to the cake batter and mix. Grease and flour two cake pans. Divide the batter between the pans and bake for 30-35 minutes. Let cool and remove from pans. Keep one cake and give one away.

As an author of heartwarming historical and contemporary romance, Sandra Ardoin engages readers with page-turning stories of love and faith. Rarely out of reach of a book, she's also an armchair sports enthusiast, country music listener, and seldom says no to eating out.

Want a FREE book?

Head over to www.sandraardoin.com/newsletter and sign up to receive the latest updates and special offers. Then download and read Sandra's historical romance *Unwrapping Hope* for free.

www.ingramcontent.com/pod-product-compliance
Lightning Source LLC
LaVergne TN
LVHW090516110826
845146LV00003B/879

* 9 7 9 8 9 9 0 5 8 4 8 0 8 *